AXLE'S ANGEL
War Angels MC

Table of Contents

Prologue
Chapter 1
Chapter 2
Chapter 3
Chapter 4
Chapter 5
Chapter 6
Chapter 7
Chapter 8
Chapter 9
Chapter 10
Chapter 11
Chapter 12
Chapter 13
Chapter 14
Chapter 15
Chapter 16
Chapter 17
Chapter 18
Chapter 19
Chapter 20

Prologue
Axle

"Alana!" I called opening the door of the café. "You here alone, doll?"

"No Axle, I'm here with a friend from work. What are you guys doing here? You don't seem like the specialty coffee types." Hammer smirked and looked around the store.

"Nah, we're not. We were across the street at the A&W getting a late lunch and Hammer saw you through the window. He said you were sitting here with an angel."

"Ha! You have no idea." Alana laughed, shaking her head. "Oh, here she comes, I'll introduce you guys." The most beautiful woman came back to the table and smiled quietly at us as she sat down. "Brooke, these are Logan's friends Axle and Hammer. Guys, this is Brooke, she teaches kindergarten at our school."

"It's nice to meet you." Brooke said politely, smiling but offered nothing more. Like the guys we are, we nodded and grunted, saying hello then turned back to Alana but I couldn't help my gaze from returning to Brooke once in a while.

"Did Lo tell you about the party at the club house Saturday?" I asked. I wasn't trying to throw my president under the bus, but I couldn't find another reason to stay where I could stare at this woman for as long as possible

"No, he never mentioned it." Alana replied, shrugging her shoulders.

"It's a kind of good bye for Demon. I'm sure Lo will tell you next time he talks to you. You should bring your friend with you." I felt like an idiot, did I sound as desperate as I felt?

"We'll see." Alana replied, smiling. We chatted for a few more minutes then did that chin jerk thing guys do and left.

***

It was the night of Demon's party and I sat at mine and Lo's usual table and watched and smiled as Lo and Alana danced and kissed. Before I could help myself I jumped up and walked across the dance floor, nudging Lo.

"Get a room!" I said laughing. When I reached the bar and looked back they were indeed leaving the dance floor, presumably to get a room. Before I could ask the prospect behind the bar for another beer a hush fell over the room. I followed the direction of everyone's gaze and saw Brooke standing in the doorway of the clubhouse.

Before anyone else could snap out of their trances I rushed over to her.

"You came!" I declared taking her hand in mine.

She nodded and smiled shyly, "I guess I did. Is Alana still here? I don't see her anywhere."

"She is here," I replied, tugging her farther into the room. "She just went back to Lo's room. Can I get you something to drink?"

"Oh, um just water." She said, still looking around the room apprehensively.

"You're not comfortable here are you?" I asked, smiling down at her and handing her the bottle of water the prospect gave me.

"That obvious huh?" She chuckled. I shrugged and stared into her crystal blue eyes. Her hair was down around her shoulders tonight and fell in straight lengths of silk to her waist. It was a white blonde that shimmered in the lowlights of the bar. "I uh don't get out much."

"It's all good," I replied, twisting a few strands of her hair around my fingers, staying close to hear her quiet voice but not too close so I didn't push myself into her comfort zone and freak her out.

I wanted nothing more than to be in her personal space but it had to be on her terms and I would bide my time. I was shocked when she asked if there was somewhere we could talk privately. Ok, shocked and elated.

I said of course and took her hand in mine, pulling her gently behind me to my room. Just as I got my door open Alana stepped out of Lo's room dressed only in his t-shirt. I shoved Brooke into my room gently and closed the door.

"Alana what the hell are you doing out here in just a t-shirt?" I demanded.

"Oh!" she exclaimed, surprised to see me in the hallway. "I was just going out to my truck to get my purse with my sketch pad."

"Go back into Lo's room; I'll get your stuff." I said waving her back inside. When she had closed the door I stuck my head into my room and told Brooke I'd be right back. She was sitting on the edge of my bed and smiled at me and nodded.

I ran back through the clubhouse hearing jeers and ribbing from the guys about being quick on the draw and getting done so fast but I just fingered them and ignored them. I grabbed Alana's shit and rushed back inside, dropping the bag just outside the door and knocking lightly. Finally I could get back to Brooke. It felt like I had left her an eternity ago even though it had been less than five minutes.

"Sorry," I said going into my room and closing my door but not latching it. She wanted privacy but I didn't want her to be nervous with me. I wanted her to know that she could leave at any time.

"That's ok, that was nice of you to do that for Alana." She said, shrugging.

"Yeah well, if I had let her run around the clubhouse in Lo's t-shirt and nothing else and he found out he'd probably kill me, especially with a party going on." I smirked. She chuckled and ducked her head. "So, privacy, any reason in particular you wanted privacy?"

Instead of answering she took a deep breath and stood walking to the door. She snapped it shut and threw the dead bolt then turned and leaned against it, looking up at me and biting her bottom lip.

"What's going on Brooke?"

"I don't know."

"What do you want?"

"You, I just don't know…"

"Did you come here tonight wanting to spend the night with me?"

"No, at least not until I saw you when I got here." She took a deep shuddering breath and took a step toward me. "When we met the other day at the café I was… intrigued by you. I didn't come here planning on getting you alone; in fact I didn't plan on coming here at all. I talked myself out of coming so many times and thought I had and then I found myself sitting in my car outside. I thought I would come in and find Alana and she would talk some sense into me but instead of finding Alana I found you. I don't know what to do, I am way out of my element but I can't seem to stay away from you."

She stepped closer to me and put her hands on my chest.

"Being here with me doesn't make sense?"

"No, it shouldn't, but I can't seem to care if it does or not." With that she rose up on her toes and kissed me. The light brush of her lips was tentative and nervous and I thought then that this beautiful creature must be a virgin but the thought was gone as soon as it came and I was lost in her.

CHAPTER 1

Brooke

I had spent the night with David. Not only had I spent the night I had sex with him. For the first time ever, I had sex . . . with David. I was no longer a 27 year old virgin. Considering I had thought I was going to join convent I'm not sure it was a good thing that I had sex with a man who wasn't my husband.

It probably was also not a good thing that he kept calling and texting and I kept ignoring him. I could imagine that would make him very angry but I didn't know what to do.

So, here I was a week later at a family bar-b-que at the clubhouse hoping beyond hope that I wouldn't see him but knowing my prayers probably weren't being answered anymore, or if they were not in the way I wanted them to be.

Thanks God, I messed with your perfect will with my free will and now I'm stuck. It's my fault, I get that but goodness, did my date with the devil have to come back to haunt me so quickly?

Not that David was the devil; he was a beautiful, wounded, haunted angel. Oh don't tell him I said he was beautiful, he would probably be insulted by that but that really is how I saw him. And he was beautiful.

He had full, thick wavy golden brown hair that hung a little too long over his ears and down his neck then curled up over the bottom of his baseball cap. He was tall, well over six feet and ripped with muscle. It wasn't fair really that temptation looked like a statue of a Greek god.

When we got here to the clubhouse I had gone over to sit with Chelle, Alana's sort of adopted daughter and the reason she met Lo in the first place. We sat and chatted about the last week of school and what she had planned for the summer as we watched all the boys play some game that was like football but totally about boys running and tackling each other with no actual point or rules.

It wasn't long before I saw Lo making his way over and I figured he wanted to talk to Chelle. I hadn't met Lo but I certainly knew who he was. I stood to give him time with Chelle and as I passed him I touched his arm but said nothing.

It was time for me to go. I had made an appearance like Alana had asked. I made my way over to say goodbye to her parents and then went to say goodbye to my friend.

"Alana, I'm going to head out." I said stepping to her side. "I will call you next week, we'll do coffee."

"Sure Brooke, I hope you had a good time today." Alana hugged me then turned back to her conversation. Before I got to the back door David stepped up to me and took my elbow in his big hand.

"Where are you going, Angel?" He demanded.

"Home, David." I replied as though that were obvious.

"Why haven't you returned any of my texts or phone calls?"

"Because David, you and I are not friends, we are not dating and I told you we couldn't be more than acquaintances through mutual friends."

"Did that night mean nothing to you?" He whispered, crowding me and getting more in my face.

I almost gave in as I took a deep breath and caught his scent. I had missed that over the last week. It was uniquely him and made me dream and want things I shouldn't want.

"That night was lovely David, but that doesn't change things. Now, I really do need to go." I patted David on the chest and walked away. He was mad but he said nothing as I left but I heard the sound of a can being crushed and he growled low in his throat.

I quickly left the building, waiting until no one could see me before I started running and tears started streaming down my cheeks. I needed to be stronger; this was not what God wanted for me, David could not be a part of my future.

Axle

I don't know what was going on with Brooke but I was not finished with her. I was not ok with just being acquaintances through mutual friends. If she really thought I was going to accept that after she gave me her virginity she was nuts.

It was the day after the bar-b-que and I had just walked into the main room. Hammer was sitting at a table with Lo and Alana and had just signed that he was waiting for Seether and I before he told us what was going on with him. I leaned back into the hallway I had just come from and hollered for Seether to get his ass out here. When we were all sitting at the table Hammer got started.

You know when my convoy hit that IED I injured my voice box and after that I sunk pretty low. He paused, rubbing his hands over his face in frustration and almost hopelessness. *When I first came back the doctors had to take out a good portion of the cartilage that makes up my voice box. That's why I can't talk loudly, the larynx doesn't make sound, it regulates pitch and volume.*

Lately mine has been so sore it felt like I was swallowing glass. That day in the gym I couldn't get a deep breath, I felt like I was choking and then when I did catch my breath the air made me choke more and cough. I passed out from lack of oxygen to my brain.

Hammer stopped signing and pushed his chair back and put his elbows on his knees then dropped his head into his hands. I could tell he was on the verge of tears but I didn't know what to do for him but wait. Finally he sat up again and brushed the tears from his cheeks that he had let fall.

In the ER that day the doctor did a couple of scans. Normally they'd have done a swab and left it at that but because of my previous injury they wanted to be extra careful. They forwarded the results of the scans to my regular doctor and Tuesday at my appointment he said what was left of my larynx would have to be removed along with a good sized tumor. They think it might be cancerous but they won't know for sure until they do a biopsy.

"Fuck brother!" I exclaimed, shoving my hands through my hair and slumping back in my chair. Alana sniffled and wiped tears from her own cheeks and left Lo's lap to kneel at Hammers side and hug him tight. When she pulled away she held his face in her hands and stared into his eyes, tears cascading down her face.

Thank you, he signed and hugged her again, burying his face in her shoulder. His shoulders rose and fell as he took deep breaths, trying to control himself.

"Hammer, what do you need?" Lo asked, gripping his coffee cup.

He sat up and looked around the table at us then patted Alana's shoulder and motioned her back to Lo.

Don't know yet. I have another appointment to find out what all is included in this surgery, and what the plan is for after. Alana, Prez told me about your cousin in the ER and I got a hold of him. Even talked to his wife, she's a psychologist; she said she would help me work through all the shit in my head.

"That's good Hammer." Alana whispered sitting in Lo's lap again and resting her head on his shoulder. We all sat quietly for a minute, lost in our own thoughts when the front door was thrown open with a bang making us all jump.

"Davy! Where the fuck are you?"

"Kat?" I answered the woman. "Is that you? What are you doing here?"

"It's her," Alana exclaimed, staring at the woman at the door dumbstruck. Lo stared at Alana like she was insane but I wasn't paying attention to them. My gaze was locked on my little sister.

"Her?" Lo demanded, "You know her?"

"Yes," Alana replied, "I mean no, I don't know her, I just saw her the other day. I was getting coffee last week when I left here and she was at the same coffee shop. She's rather eye catching, really nothing inconspicuous about her at all."

"Kat, what are you doing here?" I demanded looking down at my sister as she made a beeline to me.

"Looking for you of course, hence the reason I busted in here calling your name." Kat shook her head and pulled her rockabilly glasses off her face and pushed them on top of her head. Her hair was a crazy bright green with blue streaks and she was wearing tight jeans rolled at the cuff with chucks on her feet.

I let out a roar of frustration and rubbed my hands over my face, then tipped my head back, cocked my hip and put my hands on my waist and sighed.

"And just why were you looking for me, Kat?" I growled at her.

"Cat, the tattoo!" Alana smiled at the girl whose gaze snapped over to the other woman.

"Yeah, but with a 'K'; short for Katherine which I hate." She said squinting at Alana in concentration. "You look familiar."

She laughed, "I should, you caught me staring at you last week outside the Esquires. Nice car by the way."

"You brought the '69?" I demanded, turning to the door and stomping outside, yelling over my shoulder, "You drove my fucking mustang across the fucking country?"

I stood outside staring at the car I had missed for years. I had given the '69 electric blue mustang to Kat when I joined the army and really hadn't seen it since. I had thought her dad, my step dad, had gotten rid of it but obviously Kat had taken really good care of it. I couldn't believe she drove it all the way here from Ontario.

I pushed back into the club house and strode over to my sister, pulling her into my arms and hugging her tightly. I tucked my lips close to her ear and took a deep breath.

"Baby girl, what are you doing here?" I asked quietly, rocking her back and forth. Kat was 15 years younger than me; she has always been my baby.

"Well," she replied, pulling back from me. "Shit hit the fan. Mom and dad are getting a divorce, I told dad I wanted to come and find you since it's been five or more years with no word from you, and dad got pissed and disowned me. Mom took off with a friend who I am pretty sure is her lesbian lover but with a name like Jackie I could be wrong but who knows, so I packed the '69, which is mine by the way, and left. And here I am."

"That car is mine."

"Possession being 9/10ths of the law and all makes it mine."

I rolled his eyes at her, "When did you get here?"

"Couple of weeks ago," She answered, shrugging. "I've been staying at a dive hotel and looking for a job but so far I haven't found anyone who wants a mechanic who can't read."

"Lo," I said looking at Logan. I had always known about Kat's learning disability but never cared. I know she did, a lot and that other kids teased her for it. Whenever I was home, which admittedly was rare, I would go to her school in full dress uniform and knock some heads... figuratively of course.

"Done brother," Lo said, taking Alana's hand. "We'll leave you to figure it out."

"Come on," I said, "There's an empty room here we can move your stuff into and we're always looking for good mechanics in our garage." I hugged her again.

"So, where are you taking me for supper?" She asked smiling up at me.

"Depends, are you gonna let me drive my car?"

"Depends, if you take me somewhere good I might let you drive MY car home." Her smile was pure imp like it always was when she was a kid. God I had missed her. Looking at her now I couldn't believe how much she had grown, she wasn't a kid anymore.

CHAPTER 2
Axle

We did go to dinner and Kat told me all about mom running off with a woman named Jackie. She knew Jackie was a woman and she knew Jackie was a lesbian but mom would neither confirm nor deny that they were lovers. Kat rolled her eyes and I laughed at her.

"Like I would care, you know?" She said, shaking her head.

Then she told me about how horrible it had been with her dad the last few years. She said she had proven a hundred times over that she was smart and didn't need to be able to read but he always called her stupid and told her to get married cause popping out kids was all she was good for. Says the man who sold used cars for a living.

"So, why are you here? There's no special guy back home?" I asked her, bouncing my eyebrows at her. Yes she was my sister but she was so much younger and we had been apart for so long our relationship was more of a friendship than that of siblings.

Kat snorted, "No, definitely no special guy. The guy I was seeing was a douche and did nothing for me. He never took me out because he was embarrassed to have to read the menu for me if we went somewhere new and he hated having me around his friends and having to tell them I was a mechanic." She shook her head disgustedly.

"Actually mom told me to come. I mean I had been thinking about it anyway, but she said I should find you and live my life.

Get away from dad." She shrugged and ate her fries. "What about you, you got a special girl? You're getting on in years; you might wanna get on that soon, eh?"

"Nah, I thought maybe there was one but no. And I'm only 42; that's not getting on in years." I snorted.

"Sure, sure." She said smiling and teasing.

We finished eating and talked more about what she had been doing the last five years since I left Ontario and laughed about the shit she had done to her ex. As we were walking back to the car I threw my arms around her shoulder then started to tickle her. Before she knew what was happening I stole the car keys from her and ran, sliding behind the wheel before she could catch up.

"You're a jerk!" She laughed and panted. "You're almost twice the size of me! That was so unfair!" I just laughed at her and started the car, revving the engine and loving the sound of my baby. "Hey, I know why you're called Axle, don't you destroy my baby!"

Brooke

I couldn't believe it. I should be happy right? This is what I wanted wasn't it? I mean yes, David did just text me earlier this morning and tell me he wanted to talk and then he did call and leave a message saying he really wanted to meet in person and would I just answer the phone. And now, I see him out to dinner with another girl who looks very much more his type.

I shouldn't be upset, I should be hurt. I couldn't have him; I had decided that but that didn't mean someone else couldn't have him. Dammit, this hurt. Maybe I would get a bottle of wine and get drunk. Yeah, no I didn't need to get drunk but I did need to go home, have a good cry and a warm bath and maybe once I'd said my rosary everything would seem better. Or, at least I might be able to sleep.

I was wrong, a bath, a cry and my rosary didn't help me sleep.

Well it might have if I hadn't still been crying while I was saying the rosary. It was going to be a long summer if I was going to cry myself to sleep every night. I was in trouble; that was for sure. Thankfully today was Monday and I didn't have anywhere to be.

I worked part time at the Veterans Services building during the school year but now that summer was here my hours got bumped up to cover other people going on holidays. That was fine with me, it certainly kept me busy. I had Sundays and Mondays off so I took a long hot shower and looked through my fridge and cupboards to see what I needed to get at the grocery store.

I lived alone, having bought a small house not far from the school. I made a decent living teaching kindergarten at one of the local Catholic schools in town. I loved my job, both teaching kindergarten and teaching at the school I was at.

My house had two bedrooms which was perfect for me and a small yard. Both my parents had passed away when I was young and my grandparents had raised me. They had since died as well and I was an only child so I was alone.

I didn't need to worry about people coming over for an extended visit so my second bedroom was an office. My master bedroom wasn't huge but it was all I needed. Both of my bedrooms were on the second floor and my living room and kitchen were on the main floor.

Both my living room and my office were filled with books, both fiction and non-fiction. I loved my little house and couldn't imagine living anywhere else. It was clean and all the rooms were painted in muted blues and greens. My roommate, or rather my cat, kept me company as well as any cat could... or would.

I quickly wrote up a grocery list and headed to the local store. I walked since it was summer and I lived close enough and didn't need a lot. I kept myself on a pretty tight budget even though I didn't need to, but I firmly believed in having a rainy day fund. Of course I hadn't yet had a rainy day so my fund was rather large.

When I got home my phone was ringing on the kitchen counter. I quickly picked it up without thinking and was caught off guard when Alana's voice came through.

"Where have you been?" She demanded when I said hello. "You would not believe what has been going on here."

"Oh," I said, still not sure what to say.

"Seriously, we have to have coffee. Hammer needs to go to Vancouver to have surgery on his larynx and Axle's sister just appeared out of the blue. I think her and Hammer might end up having something going on."

"Uh,"

"I know," Alana said, "Life is so different now with Lo and his club in our lives. When are you coming out to visit again? What was going on with you and Axle at the bar-b-que Saturday?"

"Nothing, we had met by chance and talked once and I decided that we shouldn't be more than that, acquaintances that said hi. Is Hammer going to be ok?"

"Oh yeah, well we don't know yet. Turns out he's got a growth on what's left of his larynx that might be cancerous so we're all just waiting for this surgery to find out. Seriously though Axle's sister is a riot! Her name is Kat and she's got paw prints all up her back. She's so cute, about your age but not as . . . mature I guess. I couldn't believe it when she blew into the club house with her green and blue hair."

The girl from last night was David's sister! Now I felt like a real idiot, crying over it when really there was nothing between David and me and that was by my choice. I must've been quiet for too long because Alana said "Hey, you still there?"

"Oh yeah, sorry; I was just putting groceries away. Listen I've got to run or my ice cream is going to melt. I'll call you later and we'll go for coffee ok? Great, bye!" I quickly hung up before she could ask any more questions about what was really wrong with me. Gosh I felt like I was in high school again, hanging on every word my friend said hoping to hear that the cute boy liked me.

Only David wasn't a boy and he was so much more than cute. And sex was so much more than just a high school crush. What had I been thinking? I didn't have sex with random guys! Ok, so David wasn't completely random; it's not like I picked just any guy at that party to have sex with. No, I just picked the one I couldn't evacuate from my heart!

CHAPTER 3

Brooke

This couldn't be happening. It had been a week since I had talked to Alana on the phone and something was off. As in I felt strange like I was missing something. It was a Sunday and I had just gotten back from church.

It had been a lovely mass, I had taken my usual place with the choir and we sang one of my favourite hymns. The kids were super cute as usual and a couple that I had taught this past year had run to sit with me during the homily. I waved their parents off when they tried to retrieve their kids.

So, if my morning had been so wonderful why was I feeling so off? I wasn't sick; I didn't have a headache, no sniffles or even so much as a cough. What on earth was going on with me? I decided to try and ignore the feeling and grabbed one of my favourite books off my shelf and went to sit on my back porch with some sweet tea.

David had still been calling and texting and I had still been ignoring him, or at least I wasn't answering or returning his calls. I read or listened to every message and saved each one. I was really pathetic.

Why didn't I just talk to him? Really what could it hurt? Would a relationship with this man really be a bad thing? We'd already had sex and I personally thought, in my very limited experience, that it was pretty spectacular. I mean, I had been a virgin; it should've hurt right? But it didn't, it felt so good.

There had been a bit of blood yes but not a lot and David seemed to enjoy himself. He had been so sweet when he'd gotten up to dispose of the condom and came back to . . . Why didn't that sound right? Why did that memory not make sense?

David got up to dispose . . . of the . . . Oh My God!!! He hadn't worn a condom!!!

I jumped out of my chair, dumping the book that had been sitting open in my lap while I day dreamed onto the ground. I rushed up to my office and checked my calendar there.

Oh no . . . I was in so much trouble. We hadn't used a condom, the one time I had sex I forgot the condom, I wasn't on birth control and now I was late. A day late, not a big deal in the grand scheme of things but I was normally so regular that one day probably meant something.

"Shit!" I screamed at my cat. The poor creature ran out of the room and hid somewhere until his mistress stopped losing her mind. "Oh my goodness, what am I going to do? I'm not married, I had sex once and now I might be pregnant! And I swore - at my innocent cat!"

I quickly freaked out then ran downstairs, grabbed my purse and rushed out the door. I had to get to the pharmacy and get a pregnancy test. Only when I got there I stood in the aisle in front of a display of about ten different types of tests all promising the same thing; accurate results.

I looked up and down the aisle thinking I would just ask someone which test was best and easiest but wouldn't you know it the one time you wanted help no one was around.

"Shit!" I whispered to myself. I did what any sane person would do, I grabbed one of each. That's completely sane, right?

When I got to the till with my load of pregnancy tests the girl behind the counter was so bored she didn't even look at what she was ringing through. She gave me my total, I paid and ran home. I had a stick, or ten to pee on.

I read the instructions of one of the more expensive ones and it said the results would be most accurate if the first urine of the morning was used. I scowled at the test like it had just told me I would have to wait a week to find out my results.

Well, I did have ten of the stupid things. I could do a couple now and a couple in the morning. I did have to pee so really, no time like the present. I grabbed three of the tests and went to my bathroom and peed on each of them. Then I washed my hands thoroughly and left the bathroom with the tests sitting on the counter. Now that I'd done it I didn't want to see the results.

I made myself as busy as I could; cleaning and re-cleaning everything in my house. Cleanliness is close to Godliness after all. Finally I actually had to go to the bathroom again and I had no choice but to go back upstairs.

I couldn't pee in the dark and I couldn't pee with my eyes closed so I had no choice but to look at the three tests. They seemed to sit there staring at me accusingly. I peed, washed my hands and looked down at the three white sticks.

Pink plus, two pink lines and two pink lines, well hell, I was pregnant.

CHAPTER 4

Axle

I was brought to my attention that Hammer was an idiot, by none other than the man himself. It always surprised me how stupid men were. I was sure I wasn't that stupid and then one of my brother's would do something so incredibly stupid and it would make sense to me. I guess I was that stupid.

Hammer, thinking we wouldn't want to be at the hospital for his surgery just because we couldn't physically do anything. Idiot! Then I find out, last I might add, that he's dating my sister and I had to find out when he lost it after the drug dealer we were looking for held her at gunpoint.

Then he forgets the damn condom and she could be pregnant. And no, I didn't not want to know what made him make that stupid decision, as a man who had forgotten the condom I knew there were often extenuating circumstances. Those were not things I wanted to know about my baby sister.

And if it wasn't awkward enough walking into their room when she screamed at him and they were both naked, then having the talk with her about forgetting condoms and birth control and I'm done for the day, or the week.

I was still calling Brooke everyday more than once a day, I also texted her continually. As far as I knew she hadn't blocked my number but I was starting to feel like a stalker.

So here I was now, waiting for word from Alana about whether or not Brooke knew of a vet who had served in Somalia during the same conflict as Demon. It was damn frustrating that Brooke wouldn't just talk to me. If she would just explain it all to me I could maybe let it go.

We were in a meeting with the whole club talking about the shit this drug dealer was pulling with our construction sites when Alana busted into the room.

"Lo, Ord Road is on fire!" How can an entire road be on fire? We didn't wait for an explanation, just ran out of the building and jumped on our bikes.

When we got to our construction site on Ord Road we found a completely decimated trailer park and people milling about wrapped in blankets and clutching precious items. Some stood stunned watching what little they had being completely destroyed while others screamed and sobbed and clutched their children.

We all ran to the fire chief and demanded to be able to help. He looked at us like we were nuts but finally when Lo told him we had training in many areas including fire control, EMS and search and rescue the chief directed us to the area that had been set aside for first aid.

Soon we were helping in more areas and eventually all our women had shown up as well, handing out food and blankets and bottles of water. From the looks of the back of the vehicles they had bought out multiple stores in the town.

When there was nothing left to do but clean up the mess we met with the girls and started tossing the garbage left from the water bottles and food they had brought into the back of their vehicles. The girls started making plans to raise money for the people affected by this fire and we all joined in, throwing ideas out. Eventually we all made it home and into bed, some of us alone.

It was this next morning that I walked in on Kat and Hammer, her standing naked in front of the bathroom screeching his name and him in the bed completely stunned and confused, but just as naked. Then Kat was screaming at me to get out, so I did. And then talking to her about how she can't take birth control and she might be pregnant and my baby sister and one of my best friends were having sex and forgot the condom. Fuck, I'm too old for this shit.

Later that day Lo, Seether, Hammer and I were sitting in Lo's office waiting for the fed to stop by for a meeting. Hammer had gone to see Sharpie about this guy and asked him to set the meeting up. Lo was planning on making the guy uncomfortable and it certainly didn't take long.

In a small portion of the 30 minutes Lo had planned for this guy he was already yelling and throwing punches and treats. It wasn't until Kat walked in the door and called him dad then he punched her in the face that we all kind of lost it.

I had seen a picture of this guy that Demon's daughter had drawn but I didn't recognize him and I knew now that I should have. Granted he had only been in my life for three years and it had been twenty-five since I'd seen him but still, I should have known him.

"We saved him for you." I said holding out my hand when Hammer walked into the office after taking care of Kat.

"You can't do this! I'm a federal agent-" if he was going to say anything after that it was lost when Hammer's fist collided with his face and his nose exploded in a spray of blood and teeth.

"Who the fuck are you and why the fuck are you here messing with this club?" Hammer demanded getting right in the guys' face.

"You know who I am! I am Detective Sergeant Matthew Briggs. David, tell them." The agent said imploring me to help him.

"Don't look at me old man; I left you behind twenty-five years ago. Now answer the question, why are you here?" Before he answered

Briggs spit blood from his mouth, spraying Hammer's boots.

"That was dumb." One of the prospects guarding the door mumbled to the other who just nodded in quiet shock.

"Hammer, I think we need to tell his ass wipe why you're called Hammer." Lo said clapping him on the shoulder.

"I'd rather show him." The other man replied almost gleefully.

"Have at him." Lo said taking a step back and out of the range of blood splatter. He looked at me but I just shrugged as if to say 'not my problem'. So, here he sat in Lo's office while Hammer, well hammered on him. This is why the man's road name was Hammer, he hit like a 100lb sledgehammer.

He pulled his fist back and connected with the fed's stomach three times fast and then hit his face again, hard enough to split the skin over his cheek bone.

"So, answer the man's question. Why are you here?" Lo demanded quietly. Quiet angry Lo was much scarier than loud angry Lo. Briggs was starting to see that, too. He dragged a couple of deep breaths into his chest, gasping for air and wiped away some of the blood pouring out of his nose.

"David." Briggs whispered looking at me.

"What about me?" I demanded sneering at Briggs.

"I have always hated you; I thought you would join the forces and not come back. But then you did, you can't even get yourself fucking killed in a war. Then you started this stupid club and I found a way to get rid of you." Briggs coughed a few times then spit more blood onto the floor.

"We're gonna have to get that steam cleaned, Prez." Seether said from behind the video camera he was using to film the 'interview'. Better keep records and be safe and cover our asses. The rest of us snorted then turned back to Briggs.

"So you thought to take down your step son by destroying this club?" Lo said, deceptively quiet.

"That idiot Demon was so easy to manipulate. I didn't have shit on that moron. Just a few pictures of his kid and he was in my pocket." Briggs chuckled thickly.

"I saw that picture Chelle drew of him Lo, but swear to God it has been twenty-five years since I saw him." I said shaking my head in disbelief.

"Its fine Ax, I didn't recognize him either." Lo said waiving way my distress. "What else?"

"That idiot drug dealer fucked it all up. All he had to do was kill David but instead he got greedy and instead of sticking to the plan and running when I moved in with my team to arrest Demon he lost it and started shooting." Briggs coughed hard and started to pant.

"Think you broke a rib Hammer." Lo stated not at all excited or worried.

"Why'd you hit Kat?" Hammer demanded, balling his fists at his sides and I knew he was waiting for just the right answer so he could hit the asshole again.

"I didn't even know she was here." Briggs hissed. "I was trying to hit one of those idiots you had blocking the door. That girl never did have any sense, just like her mother."

Everything happened pretty fast after that. Both Hammer and I jumped at Briggs and lifted him out of his chair and slammed him against the wall, Hammers big hand crushing his windpipe

"Shut the fuck up," Hammer growled watching him turn slightly purple.

"I really do wish I could kill this piece of shit." I snarled.

"Put him down guys." Lo ordered then turned to Hammer when Briggs hit the floor. "Go get cleaned up and check on your girl. Ax, cuff this mess and put him in the back of the cage, the prospects can go with you and take him to the police station with the video. Call Sharpie to meet you all there but let him see the video before you talk to any of the cops. Cover your bases and stay safe." With that Lo turned and left the room.

I grabbed Briggs by the collar and tossed him on the floor on his stomach and pulled his arms behind his back. One of the prospects handed me a set of handcuffs and I handed Briggs off to be put in the back of one of our vans that had a cage in it. Then I pulled out my phone and shot a quick message to Sharpie to meet us at the police station.

When we got there we talked with Sharpie and showed him the video we had of the 'interview'. He said there wasn't really anything we could be held on since the man wasn't being restrained. Yes Hammer had hit him a few times but really there was nothing in the video forcing Briggs to stay in the chair, and the things he was saying were much more incriminating to him than us beating on him. There might be charges yes, but given what Briggs was admitting to we were pretty safe.

CHAPTER 5

Axle

So today, after all the excitement last night I was going to talk to the veteran that Brooke had told us about. Since it was a Tuesday I was expecting Brooke to be at school. I was sure not expecting her to be at the center, but when I walked in there she was, looking as amazing as ever.

I must have stopped to stare at her for quite some time because another worker came up behind me and watched her with me and she touched her fingers to her mouth and rushed from the room.

"I sure don't miss that." The woman said.

"What's that?" I asked without thinking.

"The morning sickness, only for poor Brooke it's all the damn time sickness." She chuckled and was about to turn away when I caught her.

"Brooke's pregnant?"

"You know Brooke?"

"Sort of, never mind I'll talk to her later. Thanks, um can you tell me where I can find Lieutenant Josh Williams?"

"Oh of course," The lady said, turning to look across the room then pointed at a middle aged man in a wheelchair sitting alone by the window. "There he is."

"Thank you," I said then made my way over and stopped at attention next to the man's chair.

We had both been out of the forces for many years but he still deserved all of my respect. I hadn't made it to officer school so this man was my superior.

"Lieutenant," I said, saluting when he looked up at me.

"At ease young man," He said chuckling. "Sit down before you give me a crick in my neck, and call me Josh." I smiled and sat down then held out my hand to shake his.

"David Bishop." I said smiling. Then I felt like the biggest idiot when Josh held out his prosthetic hook. "Fuck, sorry." I said rolling my eyes at my own stupidity.

"Don't worry about it, happens all the time." Josh said chuckling. "What can I do for you? Brooke said something about Somalia but she said that was all she knew."

"Yeah, have you ever seen this before?" I asked, handing Josh a copy of Demon's code. He looked it over for a few minutes frowning then started to nod slowly.

"Yeah, some of the guys who were part of the forces but ran black ops through a private but government funded group used this code. I haven't seen this in years. I wasn't part of that group but knew a couple of the guys, hard core for sure."

"Can you read the code?" I asked, suddenly hopeful for the first time in months.

"Not just by looking at it. I know it's made up of five different languages, two are Bravenese and Bajuni dialect from Somalia, one is Swahili, one Cushitic out of Ethiopia. The last language is the one that is more difficult to figure out because there is no rhyme or reason for it. Sometimes the guys used German, sometimes Russian or Arabic. Sometimes it depended on the content as to what language they used and sometimes the fifth language they used was a mix of multiple languages."

Josh looked over the letter I had handed him. Flipping the page over and back a few times then nodding.

"It would seem that whoever wrote this didn't want it to be too terribly difficult since they only used German for the fifth language. If you want I could have this translated for you by the weekend. Give an old crippled man something to do."

I snorted at him and smiled nodding my head. "Absolutely man, I would really appreciate it if you could translate it for me. Saves me a whole lot of work when I should be fixing cars and bikes and it keeps our computer geek from pulling his hair out. He reads code, not Swahili." I chuckled. I talked to Josh for another half an hour or so about the forces and the MC and found he was a wealth of knowledge. "You ever get a chance, you come out to the clubhouse," I said just before I left, "We would love to have you in our ranks."

"You put a sidecar on your bike I'll be out for a ride." He said laughing.

We exchanged numbers and agreed to meet up soon and I went in search of Brooke. I was so involved in what Josh was telling me I didn't see her sneak out the front door. When I got outside her car was gone.

I slammed my hands into my hair and looked up at the sky wanting to scream. That's right, big tough biker wanted to scream, like a full on psycho in the shower with a knife girl scream.

So, let's recap. I meet a great girl who I think I could really have something with. We have sex, but no not just sex. Super amazing cosmic scorch me to my feet sex. She gifts me with her virginity for fucks sakes then tells me we can only be friends but wait, I forgot the fucking condom and now I find out, months later after she's ignored and avoided me that she's pregnant.

So, either she has a boyfriend who also forgets to use condoms or

I'm going to be a father . . . and she's keeping my child from me. I couldn't help it, I let 'er rip,

"FUCK!"

CHAPTER 6

Axle

It was probably not my most shining moment when I got back to the clubhouse and immediately attacked, verbally of course, my president's fiancé but I couldn't help myself. I stormed into Lo's office past the ten or so people spread out on the couches in the main room and slammed the door.

"Did you know?!" I demanded of Alana.

"Know what?" She asked much more calmly and quietly.

"Did you fucking know she was fucking pregnant?" I yelled, no longer able to hold onto my anger.

"What?" Alana screeched, "Who's pregnant?"

"Brooke, fucking Brooke is pregnant."

"Nope, not a chance," Alana answered from Lo's lap, shaking her head. "Brooke is as close as you get to the Immaculate Conception without actually being the mother of Christ."

"What? What the fuck does that even mean?"

"The Virgin Mary was the Immaculate Conception. She was conceived without original sin so she could be the perfect vessel for Jesus." I could see that Lo was just as confused by Alana's explanation as I was. "The point is Brooke is virginal, pure, she was in a convent for crying out loud."

"She's not virginal anymore." I snorted, shaking my head. "We took care of that the night of Demon's party."

"You did what?" Alana demanded. "Fuck Axle, what the hell! Why didn't you tell me?"

"I thought she would, I didn't think she was going to completely shut me out! Haven't you noticed how sick she is? One of the other workers at the center said she's constantly sick."

"She's not at the school anymore. She put in her resignation long before we went back this fall. The only time I've talked to her in months was to ask her about that veteran. She said nothing about being pregnant or why she wasn't back at work. When I asked her she just said she had some things to figure out."

"You saw her today, you didn't talk to her?" Lo asked calmly.

"No, she rushed out of the room when I got to the center and then left before I was finished talking to Josh." I said shaking my head then I turned to Alana, "Please tell me you have her address? She won't answer my calls or my texts but she can't ignore me if I'm sitting on her doorstep."

"Yeah of course," Alana said, pulling out a piece of paper and pen from Lo's desk. She wrote quickly and handed it over. I thanked her then stomped back out to my bike. This was it, I couldn't take it anymore. If she was pregnant with my kid then I had a right to know and she was damn well going to tell me about it.

Brooke

"Coming!" I called, a little bit irritated by whoever was banging on my front door. I probably shouldn't answer it since no one had any reason to knock on my door like that but whoever it was probably wouldn't leave until I at least acknowledged they were there. "Wha-"

"What the fuck, Brooke?" David said pushing past me into my living room. "You're fucking pregnant? You know, I've been pretty fucking patient, not forcing you to talk to me, letting you take your time to realize that you needed to talk to me, no that you wanted to talk to me but then I go to the vet center and someone else tells me you're fucking pregnant."

I was so shocked he was here I stood in the open doorway with my mouth hanging as wide as the door. He sighed and took the door from my hand and slammed it shut then led me to my couch and sat me down. I watched him pace for a few minutes before he finally sighed and dipped his head back staring at the ceiling.

"Is it mine?"

"What?"

"Is the baby mine?" He demanded looking at me now.

"What do you mean, is it yours? Who else's would it be?" I demanded indignantly.

"How the hell should I know? For all I know you got me to bust your cherry then moved on the next night! Hell, it could've been that night!"

"That's disgusting," I sneered, curling my lip at him.

"Is it?" He demanded. "How would I know? You barely spoke to me before, never said a word after, waited for me to fall asleep then snuck out! In what could have been seconds the most spectacularly amazing night of my life became the most shit-tacular three months of my life."

I sighed, not really sure what to say, but knowing 'I'm sorry' just wouldn't cut it.
"So, I'm asking again, is the baby mine?"

"Yes," I sighed again, finally looking up at him. "I haven't been with anyone else. I didn't even know it was possible I could get pregnant that night. I'm sorry, I really haven't known all that long."

"You've known longer than I have." He snorted. "The party was the second last weekend of June, did you know the weekend after at the bar-b-que?"

"No, it was at least a week after that."

"So, you found out the first or second week of July and it is now the middle of September. Fucking awesome Brooke, were you planning on telling me?"

"I don't know."

"You don't know?" He demanded angrily.

"I am still freaking out!" I yelled at him, jumping off the couch sick of his attitude. "I get that you are so much older than I am and that you have probably been having sex since you were twelve! But I haven't been, I had sex once! I was in a convent for crying out loud and the one time I have sex I get pregnant! My parents are dead, my grandparents who raised me are dead, I had to quit my job because the Catholic school district can't have unmarried pregnant women teaching kindergarten and I don't blame them! We made a mistake, I made a mistake and now I'm freaking the hell out so back the hell off!"

I turned and stormed out of the living room and into the kitchen. I really wanted some sweet tea but it made me sick. I didn't have anything that could calm my nerves and I hadn't lied, I was freaking the hell out. I slammed my hands on the edge of the sink and dropped my head between my shoulders trying hard not to let the tears fall.

"Twelve?" His voice came from the doorway. I tipped my head back and chuckled morosely.

"Sure, what do I know? Maybe you were a child sex prodigy." I said sarcastically, turning towards him.

"No, sixteen but thanks for the optimism," He leaned against the door frame and watched me. "Would it be horrible of me to point out that you might know that if you'd stuck around and actually talked to me?"

"Probably, but you wouldn't be wrong," I sighed. "I'm scared David, I don't know what to do except for love this baby. I don't know where to turn and I don't know who I can lean on. I wanted to trust you and lean on you but I just don't know if I can. Alana said there was a lot of crazy stuff going on with the club and I don't want to be in the middle of that, I don't want my ... our baby in the middle of that."

"You have to know that I would keep you and our baby safe." He rasped, his voice thick with emotion.

"No, I don't have to know that," I whispered. "I knew you for all of a few hours and we fell into bed together. We didn't talk, before or after and yes, I know part of that was my fault, probably more than part of it. What I know is that you and your friends are part of a motorcycle club and the only frame of reference I have for that is the Hells Angels and what I've seen in the news."

"We're not the Hells Angels." David said adamantly, shaking his head.

"No, you're the War Angels."

"Will you let me in?"

"In what, my house? You're here. In my body? You've been there, too."

"In your heart," He whispered, finally taking a step into the room.

I shook my head on a sob and wrapped my arms around my waist. He rushed forward and wrapped his thick arms around me and held me tight. It had been so long since anyone had held me like this that I couldn't hold back the tears and the anguish.

David rocked us back and forth for a few minutes then bent and slid his arm behind my knees lifting me easily off the floor. He carried me up the stairs and into my bedroom, laying me on my bed and covering me with the blanket at the end of the bed. I thought he was leaving then but instead he took off his jacket and his boots and lay down with me, pulling me into his arms again and let me cry.

CHAPTER 7

Brooke

At some point I must have fallen asleep because the next thing I knew it was pitch black out and I was alone on the bed. I sat up groggily and immediately saw that David's jacket was still over the arm chair in the corner where he'd left it. He was still here somewhere. It shouldn't be hard to find him, it's not like I had a huge house.

I shakily got up off the bed and made my way into the bathroom. I washed my face and brushed my hair and teeth then went down stairs to face the music. How apt that when I got to the kitchen the radio was on.

David was standing just outside my kitchen door with his phone to his ear. I sighed and went to the fridge thinking I should eat something and he was probably hungry, too.

I took out two helpings of the ground beef I separated out before freezing then thought better of it and grabbed a third. I turned and David was standing right behind me and scared me, I yelped and threw the meat into the air.

"Sorry," He said softly, bending to pick up the ground beef. "Were you going to cook something with this?"

"Uh yeah, as much as I don't feel like eating I know I should for the baby . . . and I figured you'd be hungry."

"We could just order something in," He said, placing the meat on the counter. "It's not that late."

"No, this is just as easy." I said shrugging.

"You don't have a TV." David said suddenly.

"Uh no, I don't watch TV."

"Huh." He muttered, shoving his hands in the pockets of his jeans and leaning against the counter beside me as I worked. "Can I help?"

"No, I'm good." I said smiling slightly. This felt so weird, but oddly comfortable.

"So, I looked around a little while you were sleeping." He said, taking his hands out of his pockets and folding his massive arms across his just as massive chest. I smiled up at him but didn't let my gaze linger. I knew if I looked into his eyes for too long I would be completely lost. I didn't like chocolate but his deep gaze made me crave it. "I'm guessing you're going to put the baby in the office upstairs?"

"Eventually, I guess." I shrugged. I had only thought about it briefly.

"Um, can I help with that? I mean you probably don't really want to lose your office. Um, the MC has a construction company, I could have them build another small room over your porch and connect it to your bedroom, make you another office and maybe add a small bathroom if you want."

I stopped what I was doing and looked up at him, confused.

"What are you doing, David?" I whispered, suddenly feeling like I was drowning in shark infested waters.

"I'm trying to help you, Brooke. You are carrying my child; I want to be a part of that kid's life. I would prefer to do that as his mother's husband but I know we have a long way to go before you even consider that. For now I would like to do that as its mother's friend." He sighed heavily and straightened up from the counter, turning to face me. "I spent the last almost three months not pushing you and missed almost three months of my child's life. You are completely freaked out and scared and I get that, I really do understand that, but if you had just talked to me in the first place we could've had this all straightened out."

"This is –"

"No Brooke, this is just the beginning and it's three months late. I'm done waiting for you, I'm pushing now. I'm not going to force you to marry me or sleep with me again or date me or anything like that but I am going to force you to give me a chance. I don't love you, I can't yet I barely know you and sure, that probably means we shouldn't have had sex but we did and now here we are."

"Yeah but –"

"No, no buts. I'm 42 years old, two of my best friends have found their happily ever after, one of them with my baby sister, and yes I'm fucking jealous. Do I think I could find that with just anybody? Sure, probably, maybe I don't know. But not just anybody is pregnant with my baby. Please Brooke, please give us a chance."

I stared into his eyes for so long I forgot that I hadn't answered him. Finally I nodded at him, but otherwise didn't move. His big warm hands came up and bracketed my cheeks and he kissed me on the forehead and then he hugged me tight.

"Are you sure I can't help with dinner?" I had no words so I just nodded again. "Ok, then I'm gonna run out and grab you a TV, I've got an extra one at the clubhouse. I'll be back in thirty minutes; that ok with you?" Again I nodded but this time I frowned up at him. "Exhibition game tonight babe, gotta train our kid on the rights and wrongs of hockey early."

And with that he was gone, presumably to return... with a TV.

Axle

I rushed out of Brooke's house and jumped on my bike. I was suddenly feeling lighter than air. I had called Lo earlier to tell him what was going on and not to expect me around much.

He told me what was going on with the carnival and I told him I would do whatever he needed me to do. It seemed I would be in the damn dunk tank for at least part of the day.

I rode my bike back to the clubhouse and parked it in the garage we all used. I ran inside, quickly packed a bag, unhooked my TV and android box and rushed back out to my truck. I was back on the road in less than ten minutes and on my way back to my life. At least that's what I hoped; only time would tell.

When I got back to Brooke's I grabbed everything from my truck and rushed in the front door. Thankfully she hadn't decided she couldn't do this and locked the door. She was however sitting on the couch looking completely petrified. I dropped my bag and carefully put the TV down and walked over to her. Sitting on the coffee table in front of her I took her hands in mine and made her look up at me.

"Brooke baby, look at me." She looked first over at my bag and my TV then back at me frowning. "I'm not moving in, I'm just afraid to give you a chance to lock me out again. I promise you I've only brought a few things for a few days and I will sleep on the couch."

"You can't sleep on the couch; it's an antique and completely uncomfortable." She mumbled, still frowning. "You can sleep in my bed but I don't think I'm ready for anything else."

"That's ok baby, I don't want anything else." She cocked her eyebrow at that and I nodded sheepishly. "Yeah, you're right I want a whole lot more than that but I'm not going to take it. When you're ready to take it I will give it to you but you are in control. You are completely in control of all of this but I'm not going away. You can't get rid of me."

"Come on," She said chuckling and standing, "Dinner should be ready."

"Excellent," I said, jumping up to follow her into the kitchen. "I'm starving."

"Will you tell me about your club while we're eating?"

"Of course sweetheart, anything you want to know." It was an easy thing to promise since we really didn't have any secrets. We weren't a typical MC, we weren't a 1%ers club and we kept everything we touched completely legal. She asked a lot of questions as we ate and I was happy to answer them all. "Brooke, this spaghetti is amazing." I said at one point completely honestly.

"I like to cook, it's nice to have someone to cook for instead of just for myself." She shrugged and wiped her lips with her napkin. "Tell me about all this trouble Alana says you've been having."

"Well," I sighed as I swallowed my last bite, "It's kind of a shit show to tell you the truth. And it's a long story, you sure you want to hear it all?"

"Yes, I am sure that I want to hear it all."

"All right then let's go into the living room. You can get comfortable on the couch with a blanket and I'll tell you about it while I set up the TV."

"Multitasking?" She asked cheekily.

"And I'll even do the dishes later."

"Pfft, there aren't any, I clean while I cook. But thanks for offering." She smiled and followed me into the living room. Good to my word I got her comfortable on the couch with a blanket and moved an end table to put my TV on.

"Let's see, about six or seven months ago one of our members got on the wrong side of a drug bust. No, he was not involved in the actual drugs or the deal and neither were we, we didn't even know about it. Turns out some federal agent from back East got a hold of Demon and bribed him into getting involved with this small-time drug dealer in exchange for his daughter's safety. Demon had demons, shall we say and instead of coming to Lo and I with this shit he went off on his own. Of course he just didn't go off but left a trail of breadcrumbs for us to follow."

Demon was Michelle's dad right?" Brooke asked.

"Yup," I said, lifting my TV onto the table and following the cord back to the wall outlet. "The Fed had pictures of Chelle and threatened her to make Demon do what he wanted. Well, the drug deal went back and Demon raced out of the bust and ended up crashing his bike and dying."

"The party that night was for him."

"Uh huh, so besides this Fed we couldn't get a hold of if our lives depended on it, which they actually kind of did, we also had this small time dealer on our asses." I hooked the android box up to the TV and plugged it in as well then sat with Brooke on the couch. "So Demon's dead, our lawyer is meeting with the Fed but not getting any answers and the dealer is holding my sister at gunpoint. Meanwhile Hammer is getting surgery on his voice box because it was damaged in an IED attack in Afghanistan and Lo and Alana are doing their whatever they're doing."

Brooke snorted at that but smiled, obviously happy for her friend.

"Right? So my sister just showed up one day a few months ago, the morning after the bar-b-que actually. Just out of the blue and the door flies open and there's Kat standing there with her blue and green hair yelling at me to get my ass out of wherever I was hiding. Then she hooks up with Hammer and now they might be pregnant."

The whole time I talked I was messing with the remote and the

TV and trying to get it all set up. When I got to the spot to put in her wifi password I handed her the remote and she keyed in the code.

"So, none of us knew that Chelle existed until Alana busted into the clubhouse and ripped Lo a new one. That was something to see, let me tell you."

"That sounds like Alana; she's a very fierce mama bear." Brooke chuckled.

"I'd say. So we went through all of Demon's stuff again but looked more closely at things and started figuring things out. All that led us to a storage unit that Demon had set up like an office and we found even more stuff, including a letter written in code that Seether couldn't crack no how."

"Seether?"

"Computer geek at the club." She nodded in understanding and I went on. "So that's what I was doing at the center today. Alana had called you about a vet who had been stationed in Somalia right? Turned out this code was something the guys in a black ops group used over there and Josh might actually be able to crack it for us."

"Josh is a good guy, so troubled. I'm glad he can help you, he really needs to feel useful."

"I can see how that would be hard being in a wheelchair, no legs and only one arm."

"Yeah, when he came back from wherever his last deployment was he was broken mentally. The physical injuries were bad enough but the emotional ones were the worst."

"They are for most of us." I whispered nodding, then continued with my story. "Well, it turns out that the fed is actually Kat's dad -."

"Wait, Kat's your sister, her dad? But not your dad?"

"Nope, my step-douche, my mom married him when I was about fifteen and Kat was born soon after that. I don't think it was a full nine months though. So I stuck around for three years because I had to but as soon as I turned eighteen I joined the armed forces with Lo. I was back off and on and then a couple weeks before Kat showed up at the clubhouse our mom packed up her shit and left. Told Kat to come find me and get away from her dad, get on with her life."

"Step-douche huh? Sounds like a great relationship."

"Huh, you don't even know the half of it. So Kat's dad had always hated me, I don't even know why and he really had hoped I would die overseas, only I didn't and then a couple of years after Lo and I got home for good we came out here and started the club. So the douche decided this was a good way to kill me. Thing is, we always thought he was a used car salesman, he fooled a lot of people."

I pointed the remote at the TV and searched through my saved channels looking for hockey. Brooke sat beside me quietly for a while then shifted so she was leaning against me. I lifted my arm so she could snuggle against my chest and held her tight to me.

"So, educate me on this thing called hockey." She said putting a hand on my stomach. I looked down at the top of her head and smiled. I finally felt like I had a home.

CHAPTER 8
Brooke

I was really at a loss. It had been a week since David had shown up at my house and declared he wasn't leaving. He had slept in my bed every night doing nothing more than holding me, all night long.

In the morning we would get up and he would take a shower while I made breakfast, we'd eat together and chat about our day then he would kiss my forehead and leave, telling me to text or call him if I needed anything.

I had only done so once. I needed something for supper that I couldn't get at the store close enough to walk to. I could have driven but I had an insane feeling like I needed to test him. I called him and asked for something quite ridiculous.

He didn't ask questions or demand why I needed it, just asked me to text him exactly what I needed. When he got home he was carrying two grocery bags full of stuff I didn't need or want.

"I think I found what you wanted at the store you said, but I wasn't sure so I grabbed a few things that were similar." I stared at him in shock.

Half the stuff he'd brought home I didn't know what I was going to do with it so I froze it then started looking up recipes on the internet so none of it would go to waste.

Today was Saturday and David was involved in the toy run that the club was doing to raise money and collect donations for the families affected by the fire on Ord Road. Really, none of what happened could be blamed on the club but that didn't matter.

They felt that their company and club had affected the town in a negative way and they had to fix that. So, today they were doing the toy run and next week they would be doing the carnival. David had mentioned that I was more than welcome to come by the clubhouse and help out in any way I wanted but I still didn't feel comfortable being there.

I hadn't talked to Alana in quite some time and I know that David had told her I was pregnant. I hadn't told her and I had pretty much shut her out of my life because I was so freaked out about it all.

I had quit my job at the school because I knew the archdiocese would have a problem with an unmarried pregnant woman teaching little kids. Not really the image they want to portray and really they were right. People made mistakes for sure and shouldn't be punished for those mistakes but really, I had signed a contract saying I would live a Catholic lifestyle.

My major problem now was finding the words to tell David that I wanted more. I didn't know how to tell him he was driving me crazy, sleeping beside me but not really touching me, holding me but going no farther than to kiss my forehead.

I was frustrated and dare I say I was completely sexually frustrated. Was it pregnancy hormones? Maybe but I had found David completely irresistible before I was pregnant so really, it could just be David. Just then the object of my frustration walked in the front door.

"Hey Angel, I'm just going to grab a shower and I'll be right down." He said kissing my forehead, my forehead again, and ran up the stairs.

I didn't even look up from the book I was pretending to read before he was gone from the room. That was it, I was done with the forehead kissing! I jumped up off the couch and followed him up the stairs.

By the time I got there he was already in the shower. Since I only had one bathroom we never bothered to lock the door. Quietly I opened the door and slipped in. I could see him through the steam from the shower and the clear door, starting to get nervous.

I took a deep breath and tossed my nervousness away and whipped my shirt over my head before I could change my mind then shoved my pants down my legs. I quickly slid the shower door open and climbed into the tub.

"What-?"

"Shh," I said, taking David's mouth in a kiss that I hoped conveyed how absolutely frustrated I was.

"Angel, you don't have to do this."

"David, shut up, you've been making me crazy for the last week. I don't know if it's hormones or you or me or I don't know but you've been driving me nuts. I just need you to make love to me, please."

He stared at me for a few seconds frowning, trying to make up his mind whether he should push me away or not. Finally he slid one of his hands around my neck and pulled me to him, slipping his other hand around my waist.

"Are you sure Angel?"

"Please David? I don't know how else to ask, I –"

Before I could say anything else his mouth was on mine and his tongue was licking past my lips. I moaned and lifted my hands to his chest, pushing one up into his hair and flicking his nipple piercing with the other.

When I had first seen David's piercing I had been equally intrigued and frightened by it. I couldn't help but wonder what I had gotten myself into but when I began playing with it and I saw how that affected him I quickly relaxed.

When I flicked his piercing this time he gasped and pulled me closer to him. His hand around my waist slid down and cupped my ass, pulling me up on my toes. I whimpered when his tongue left my mouth and he nibbled on my lips.

"I don't want to do this in the shower." He said breathing heavily. "I want to worship you in your bed."

"Our bed David," He was so tall I had to tip my head almost all the way back to look into his eyes. The look there was so intense I thought it was going to burn me alive.

"Our bed," He turned and shut the water off then came back to me and lifted me, wrapping my legs around his waist and carrying me across the hall to my room.

He stopped beside my bed and let me slide down his body, his thick cock nudging between my legs making me whimper again.

"Fuck Angel," David said latching onto my throat and sucking, "This is gonna be hard and fast, you gotta tell me if I hurt you. I've needed you so much I'm gonna lose control so fast."

"David, do we need a condom?" He stopped and pulled away from me.

"I don't know, do we? I don't know anything about sex and pregnancy and babies."

"Not for the baby, the baby will be fine if you have no diseases."

"You think I might have a disease?"

"I don't know David; this is something we never talked about. I don't know what your sexual habits are. Do you have a lot of sexual partners? Do you often forget the condom like we did?" I'd messed up; I saw it as soon as those words left my mouth.

"Until you I have never forgotten the condom. I do not have a lot of sexual partners; I hadn't been with anyone for close to a year before you and I'd been tested before you. I haven't been with anyone since you. I only wanted you." He sighed and turned away, making to leave the room.

"David wait," I called, reaching for him.

"What Brooke? You want me or you don't. If you really want me you have to trust you. Our history notwithstanding I would do nothing to hurt you. When you finally decide that you want all of me and can trust all of me let me know."

With that he was gone, I stood in my bedroom completely naked until I heard the front door slam and his bike start up and roar away.

Then I wrapped my arms around me and crumpled to the floor and sobbed.

CHAPTER 9

Axle

I was wrong. As soon as I slammed the front door I knew I was wrong. I should've stayed and talked to her. Fuck I could be stupid sometimes, but I was hurt and angry.

I knew she had been testing me in the little things she would say or do. I didn't think asking about a condom was a test, but it still hurt that she still didn't really trust me.

I had gone to the clubhouse and had a beer with the guys. They were celebrating the success of the toy drive and when I saw Kat tell Hammer to meet her in their room I knew it was time for me to grow the fuck up and go back to Brooke. I had already been gone for far too long and I wasn't going to fix what was wrong sitting at a bar and drinking beer.

I hurried back to the house and ran in calling Brooke's name but got no answer. All of the lights were off but I had only been gone an hour or so and it was only 7 so I doubted she went to bed.

"Brooke! Angel, where are you?" Not like it was a big house. I ran out to the back porch where she liked to sit but she wasn't there. "Brooke!" I called again stomping up the stairs.

I was really starting to get worried now; why wasn't she answering me? When I threw the door to her room open I was shocked to find her sitting in the window seat with a blanket wrapped around her. It looked like she hadn't gotten dressed from when I left.

She didn't look at me when I walked into the room and she didn't move when I kneeled beside her. I tried to take her hand but she buried it deeper into her blanket.

"Brooke baby, look at me." I don't know if she ignored me or chose not to hear me but she didn't move. "Brooke, I'm sorry, I was an ass. I shouldn't have gotten mad. Please talk to me baby."

Still she ignored me and I couldn't take it anymore. I shrugged out of my jacket and picked her up. She fought me a little but she was no match against me. I carried her to the bed and laid her down then kicked off my boots and lay down next to her.

She tried to roll away from me to the far side of the bed but I grabbed her and pulled her back into my chest. Before I could say anything more she broke and started sobbing.

"I'm sorry baby. I shouldn't have gotten mad; I had no right to get angry. Please talk to me Angel." I whispered nonsense in her ear; telling her I was sorry and stupid and could she please forgive me. Eventually she fell asleep and I turned her to face me and held her tight. God I was an ass.

Brooke

I don't know what woke me but I was suddenly so hot. I shifted slightly, breathing in the scent of David and tensing, trying to push away from him without waking him but his arms tightened around me.

"Stay Angel baby," He murmured, burying his face in my hair. "I'm so damn sorry."

I relaxed slowly and burrowed into his chest again. I glanced at the clock behind him and saw it was barely six in the morning. Sunday morning, I had to go to mass and I usually went to the nine am mass but it was time to talk to Alana. I would sleep longer then go to the eleven am mass so I could catch her.

I hadn't planned on sleeping much later but it was after nine when I finally rolled out of bed. David was gone but I knew he was still in the house somewhere. When I stepped out of my room I heard the shower running and rushed down stairs.

I wasn't going to make that mistake twice. I was in the kitchen making a cup of tea when I heard his boots on the stairs. I turned and put his coffee pod in the Keurig I had bought for him when he first started staying here and brewed him a cup. The machine hissed and chugged as he stood in the doorway watching me.

"Brooke?" I glanced at him over my shoulder and smiled a little but didn't turn away from the window. He took a deep breath and opened his mouth to say something but I cut him off.

"I'm sorry." I said quickly. "I shouldn't have questioned you."

He sighed heavily and shook his head, walked over to me and turned me into his arms.

"You're allowed to question me. I'm sorry I got mad, you should've questioned me. If you were my sister or heaven forbid my daughter I would want you to question those things. I had no right getting mad and storming out of here."

"I just don't know what I'm doing." I said, wrapping my arms up under his arms and over his shoulders.

"I know, and honestly neither do I." He hugged me tight again then pulled back and tilted my chin up and kissed me gently on the mouth.

"Will you come to mass with me today?" I asked and watched as his eyes got huge and he seemed to gape like a fish.

"Uh, ok? I don't remember the last time I went to church."

"It's ok if you don't want to go." I said shrugging. "I go every Sunday, often on weekdays and I really enjoy mass. Usually I go to the earlier mass but you kind of wouldn't let me go this morning and

I decided I needed to talk to Alana so I would go to the mass she usually goes to."

I was rambling, I knew it but I couldn't stop myself.

"Of course I'll go with you." David said seriously. "I want to be part of your life, if that means going to church then I will go. And probably I will either enjoy myself or learn something."

I smiled up at him and kissed him lightly then went up to shower. I think this was going to be a momentous day.

***

Oh my goodness, this was a disaster! What the hell was I thinking asking David to go to mass with me? I lived close to the Cathedral in downtown Kamloops so I was able to walk. David took my hand as we walked and asked questions about what he should expect. Really, right up until we walked in the front doors of the church the day was perfect. And then Church Lady spotted me.

"Well," she said rushing over to me and tightly grasping my elbow. Tight enough, that is that I winced and knew I was going to bruise. Luckily David was distracted by the opulence of the Cathedral, even though it was very plain compared to some churches. "You weren't at mass this morning; I thought something had happened to you."

"Uh no, Connie we just decided to sleep in this morning."

"We?" Dammit!

"Uh yes, Connie this is David, my –" my what? Shit!

"Fiancé," David said for me, holding his hand out to shake Connie's.

She looked at his hand like she saw something disgusting then held her own hand out like she was the queen. David grabbed her hand in his firm grasp and shook it like the blue collar worker he was. The amazing, spectacular, down to earth blue collar worker that he was.

"Pleased to meet you, Connie was it?"

"Fiancé, so then you aren't married and you're sleeping in together?"

"Yes Connie," I said aggravated, "David stayed over late and had been drinking and I didn't want him to have to drive home after a beer so he slept on the couch." David it seemed could barely control his laughter. I nudged him with his elbow but his shoulders just shook harder. "Well, if you'll excuse us, this mass is usually quite busy and we were hoping to sit with Alana and her family."

I knew I was being snarky but I couldn't help it. I blamed it on the hormones. Usually I could handle Connie and her overbearing holier than thou ways but for some reason today I just couldn't take it. Maybe it was because she was being rude to David?

"Yes, she and the boys and her mom and dad are up close to the front there." Connie said, pointing delicately.

"Oh, is Lo here with her?" David asked looking over the congregation.

"Who?"

"Logan Winters," David answered, looking back at Connie. "Her fiancé?"

"Oh, the biker, yes he is here as well. You know Brooke; you might want to speak to her about that man. I don't know that he's the best role model for the boys."

I felt my eyes widen as though they were going to jump out of my head and David turned away from us pretending to look at some of the pamphlets that were stacked at the back of the church.

"Well, since Mr. Winters' is the president of the club that David is the vice president of, I don't think I'm the best person to talk to her about that. Have a good day, Connie." I said narrowing my gaze at her before I took David's hand and pulled him to the front of the church.

He squeezed my hand and I looked up into his smiling face and I couldn't help but roll my eyes. We found a place in the pew right behind Alana and Lo and David poked his friend in the shoulder.

Logan turned around surprised to see David, who nodded to the side at me. Logan smiled at me and shook his friend's hand then nudged Alana to look behind them. When she turned her eyes teared up and she covered her lips with her fingertips. She turned right around and hugged me tight.

"I missed you." She whispered in my ear. "We got lots to talk about."

She winked and turned back around. Her youngest Drew snuck out of the pew and rounded the end to sit between David and I then started signing so fast I almost couldn't keep up, but David could and did. Soon the mass started and Drew quieted down.

David sat quietly and followed all the actions and postures that the people around him did and when it was time for Communion Drew showed him to fold his arms over his chest so the priest would know to give him a blessing. David nodded and gave the little boy a thumbs up then stepped out of the pew and motioned me in front of him.

After mass Alana turned to me and hugged me tight again.

"Let's get brunch." She said, looking from me to David to Logan. I shrugged because this was pretty much exactly what I wanted to happen but looked to David with a question in my eyes.

"I'm all for it." David said shrugging and Logan agreed.

"Mom, dad, do you want to join us?" Alana asked her parents.

"Oh no dear," Joann said. "Why don't we take the boys home and help them get their homework and what not ready for school tomorrow."

"Thanks mom." Alana said and hugged her parents. "Why don't we walk up to the diner on the next block?"

"Sure, that sounds great." I said smiling. The guys agreed and we all left. The guys walked ahead of us talking about something but I wasn't paying attention to them. "I'm sorry."

"What? What for?" Alana demanded.

"For not coming to you and telling you what was going on." I shrugged.

"Sweetheart, I'm pretty sure you were freaked the hell out, am I right?" I snorted and nodded. "I know I would be if I were you. I wish you had come to me but I totally understand why you didn't. Don't worry about it."

I smiled at her and hugged her to me as we walked. I caught David sneak a glance back at us and smile.

CHAPTER 10

Axle

Everything recently had been so great. The garage had been great, there hadn't been any more threats from Kat's dad or the drug dealer and the carnival to raise money for residents of Ord Road was a huge success.

We had raised $100,000 total and now Lo was meeting with Tank to figure out what we needed to do with the city to get started on rebuilding homes. What had burned was a trailer park and the homes there were not extravagant but they were people's homes and they did need to be replaced.

I had also gotten a message from Josh at the center that he was finished the translation of Demon's code. He said it had taken him a lot longer than he had planned but it was ready when I was. Brooke said she watched him every day she was at the center and he was always hard at work on it.

The only thing missing in our lives was sex. And really I didn't miss sex so much as I missed being intimate with Brooke. I know she felt the same way, I could tell by the way she watched me when I came in a room or how she blushed when I caught her watching me.

I also knew she would never make the first move again after what happened the last time. I decided that I was going to take her to bed as soon as possible, and not just take her to bed, but really make her mine. I had a deep urge to worship her and love every inch of her.

She was also growing round with our baby. She was absolutely glowing now that the morning sickness had finished and she had a little more energy. I held her tight every morning after my alarm went off, not wanting to let her go and then every night we cuddled on the couch and I held her tight there, too.

She made us supper and eventually she went up to bed while I watched hockey or football or whatever was on until I was too tired to do anything but hold Brooke and sleep.

"Hey man," I said to Josh as I walked up to his usual table in the center.

"Axle, how's it hanging?"

"Long and straight man, why haven't we seen you out at the clubhouse yet?"

"Haven't heard if you've gotten that side car yet!" Josh said laughing.

"What have you got for me?" I asked sitting across the table.

"Well, I don't know who this Demon fellow was but he was into it up to his eyeballs." Josh said, shaking his head. "So let me explain his code to you. Like I said before it's a mix of Bravanese, Bajuni, Swahili, Cushitic and in this case an obscure dialect out of northern Russia. That's why it took me so long to figure this out. This particular dialect is from the area around Vologda.

"So when written it's Bravanese, Bajuni, Swahili, Cushitic, Bravanese, Bajuni, Swahili, Cushitic, Bravanese, Russian, Bajuni, Swahili, Cushitic and so on. Every tenth word is in Russian. Sometimes the order of the first four languages is rearranged but this is the most common."

My eyes must've been wide because Josh just laughed at me. "It's not that hard once you get the hang of it." He said just as Brooke strolled over to us.

"Hi guys, do you mind if I join you?" She asked, putting her hand on my shoulder.

"That's up to Axle; these are his high priority high security papers." Josh said, winking at me.

"It's fine Angel, come sit here with me." I said pulling her into my lap.

"David stop, I'm too heavy." She protested but didn't push too hard.

"You stop it; you'll be nine months pregnant and still not be too heavy for me." I said sniffing her hair.

"So that's how it is, eh?" Josh asked, shaking his head. "And here I thought I still had a chance."

"Sorry Josh," Brooke said shrugging, "David is already fifteen years older than me, I think anything more than that would be stretching it."

"Nonsense," the older man insisted. "I'm still spry in my old age!" We chuckled together and Josh finished telling me about the code and what it all said. To say I was surprised by what Josh told me would be a huge understatement.

"Fuck," I groaned, leaning my head back against the chair I was sitting in. "I gotta get this back to Lo and the club. Thanks Josh," I said holding out my hand to shake his, this time my left hand so he could actually shake my hand. I took Brooke's hand once we'd said goodbye to Josh and made her walk me to the door. "What are your plans now Angel?" I asked turning to her and pulling her into my arms.

"I'm actually done for the day." She said wrapping her arms around my waist and tilting her face up to me. "I haven't been feeling very good today, I've got a headache and I can't take anything for it so my boss sent me home."

"You okay Angel baby?" I asked, cupping her cheek in my hand.

"Yeah I'm ok. I'm just going to go home and have a nap I think." She said then pushed up on her toes and kissed me again. I couldn't help it; I opened my mouth over hers and pushed my tongue in, licking the roof of her mouth. She gasped and I took advantage, pulling her against me and kissing her harder.

"Mmmm, fuck baby," I whispered dropping my forehead against hers. "I gotta have you, soon. Can I have you please?"

She stared up at me, her eyes wide then she nodded. "Ok, I want you David I'm just scared but I do trust you." I kissed her gently again, holding her sweet body to mine, feeling the tiny bump of our baby between us. I patted her on the butt and pushed her gently towards her car.

"Go home, get some rest. I'll be home as soon as I can." I said, watching as she got in her car and drove away. I sighed and dropped my chin to my chest. God I hoped this shit with Demon would end soon. I climbed on my bike and rode out to the clubhouse, not looking forward to showing Lo what Josh had uncovered.

When I got to the clubhouse I went straight to Lo's office, telling the guys I saw along the way that we needed a meeting now. The few that were there jumped up and hurried to the meeting room, pulling out phones to text other members.

"Lo," I said sticking my head in his office doorway. "I got it, some of the guys that are here are waiting in the meeting room but I can't wait for the rest to get here. I gotta give you all this and then go."

"Sure," Lo jumped up out of his chair and followed me into the meeting room. We waited another 5 minutes until everyone was finished texting whoever and was paying attention. "Axle?"

"I met with Lieutenant Josh Williams a couple of weeks ago. He knew Demon's code, or at least of it and could translate it. We all know that Demon served in Somalia in the '90s and a black ops group came up with this code. It's made up of four main languages and one or more that are switched out depending on the situation. We're looking at Bravanese, Bajuni, Swahili, Cushitic and in this case Russian." The guys all looked kind of confused and I didn't blame them.

"So, when writing the code, every tenth word is Russian. B,B,S,C,B,B,S,C,B,R,B,S,C and so on." I said using just the first letters of the different languages. Some of the guys nodded like they understood and other's just shrugged like it didn't matter. "So Josh translated it for us, too. Lo, you wanna read it, or do you want me to?"

"You do it."

I took a deep breath and started;

> To anyone reading this, Lo I hope it's you. I have a daughter. I've always known about her but have told no one she existed. I was always afraid that my past would hurt her in some way.
> Now it has. Michelle had always lived with her mom on the island. Jen and I have always been a couple, I loved that woman with my whole being but when she got pregnant I knew I couldn't keep her and the baby, Michelle safe enough. I was there when Michelle was born, she is named after me and has my last name but she knows nothing about me. There is a letter in a safe deposit box that will explain everything to her. Jen dying is a freak accident was definitely never in the plans. When the social workers found Jen's will and it had me listed as Michelle's uncle and only living relative they contacted me to take her. I knew if I didn't take her she'd go to foster care and I couldn't have that. When Briggs contacted me he showed me pictures of Michelle that noone should have had and yes, I feared for my daughter's life and

safety. Briggs did not say a word to me about the club. As far as I knew at the time he only wanted to take down the dealer. After talking to the dealer a bit the dumb shit let it slip that Briggs was after the club. I have one more meeting with this dealer next week. Neither he nor Briggs know that after that meeting their little game is up and the club and Michelle will be safe.

Lo, I wanted to come to you and tell you all of it, every little bit but I was scared for Michelle. I'm sorry, I hope you understand. Hopefully you will never have to see this letter, but if you do it means something happened and my plan didn't work and I'm dead. Take care of Michelle. All of the info you will need to take down Briggs is in that box at the bank. All the information you'll need is locked away in a locker at the bus depot. Michelle has the key but probably doesn't realize it. Lo, you'll need her to get the box open. Don't forget, take care of her for me. There's also some very sensitive information in there about a corporation called Canadian Multi-National Security Services. It's a black ops group funded by the government and completely off the books. I was a part of this group in Somalia. It was being involved in what that group did that broke me. If they're still operating there's enough there to take them down and lock away more than a few high level politicians. If you choose to expose CMNSS be careful, they are far past ruthless and will do anything to keep their secrets.

Take Care, Michael "Demon" Edwards.

Everyone sat quietly for a few minutes, staring at me. Finally Lo spoke;

"So, I guess we gotta get Chelle and get to the bus depot."

"Do what you need to, brother, I gotta get home to Brooke." I said standing. Lo nodded then caught my arm.

"Can this shit at the bus depot and the bank wait until tomorrow?" He asked looking up at me.

"Might as well, we can't get to any banks today anyway, it's gonna be too late by the time we get the stuff from the bus depot." I said shrugging.

Lo nodded again and said goodbye. I rushed out of the room and then out of the clubhouse, rushing home to Brooke. I didn't know if she was feeling all right or if she was just tired, but I needed to get back to her and hold her tight.

I was tired of dealing with all of this shit with Demon, I just wanted life to go back to the way it was, or at least how it was but with Brooke, Kat and Alana. I was as ecstatic as a biker could be to have his sister back in his life and happy with Brooke. Alana made my brother happy and that's all that mattered.

I made it to the house and quietly went inside, just in case Brooke was sleeping. I found her this time in the kitchen surrounded by warm, fresh out of the oven chocolate chip cookies.

"Angel, what are you doing?" I asked looking around at the cookies covering every surface in the kitchen.

"I had a craving for chocolate chip cookies, but now that I've made them I don't want them."

"Are there any more in the oven?"

"No, I just pulled out the last batch and turned the oven off." She sighed, brushing her hair back from her face.

"Good, let's go."

"Go, go where?"

"To bed, I've had a rough day and I just want to hold you, preferably naked and hopefully leading to more than just holding."

CHAPTER 11

Axle

"Oh, yes please." She breathed looking at me with such longing my cock sprung hard and painful against my zipper. I took her hand and dragged her behind me up to our room. As soon as we got through the door I turned on her and kissed her hungrily.

Brooke whimpered and ran her hands up my chest and into my hair. I turned us and started walking her back towards the bed, pulling our clothes off as we went. It wasn't long before she stood in front of me in nothing but a bra and panties. My shirt was gone but I was still wearing my pants.

Brooke stood and stared up at me, her eyes big and the blue of her irises so clear. She slowly reached out for my belt buckle, fumbling with it until it let go then she pulled on my button and fly and shoved my jeans down my legs.

I reached up and pulled the straps of her bra down her arms, letting them fall at her elbows then pushed her gently back on the bed crawling over her. Before I could settle myself between her legs she nudged my shoulder and pushed me to my back.

I was still wearing my underwear and it was tented straight up in the air. She kneeled beside me looking me over and licking her lips then reached back and undid the clasp on her bra. Brooke tossed the bra across the room and leaned over me, sucking my nipple ring into her mouth. I moaned and cupped her head, holding her to me as she teased me. I reached up with my other hand and teased her nipple, drawing a gasp from her lips.

Brooke kissed a trail down my chest and swirled her tongue in my belly button then nipping at the skin just under the waistband of my boxer briefs. I growled when she dipped her tongue below the waistband and started tugging them down with her hands.

"Brooke wait," was all I got out before my cock sprang free and she was licking me. "Oooohhhh my God!" I moaned. She was completely unschooled but I swear it was the best blow job of my life. "Lick around the head Angel . . . that's it, take it in your mouth as far as you can . . . mmmm, yes baby . . . like that Angel . . . wrap your hand around the base and squeeze."

Everything I said she did and she learned very quickly how to please me. It didn't take long before I was on the brink of losing control and had to take over.

I jack knifed up and rolled her under me, kissing her hard. My hands moved over every inch of her, leaving a scorching path that my lips followed until I got between her legs. I licked over her panties and found them soaking wet. I bit her gently through her underwear and laughed when she shrieked.

"Baby, does sucking me off get you excited?" I asked, playing with the edges of her panties.

"Uh huh," she said panting and nodding. I slid a finger under her panties and petted her pussy lips, making her moan and arch her neck, pushing her head into the bed.

"I'm gonna eat you Angel baby." I said pulling her panties down her legs, "I can't wait to taste you Angel."

She whimpered and tried to clench her knees shut but I wouldn't let her. I used my broad shoulders and pushed her thighs apart, exposing her sweet pussy to me. She whimpered again as I sucked on the sensitive skin around the juncture than levered off the bed when my tongue finally connected with her clit.

"God you taste good Angel baby! I can't do this for long, I gotta be inside you or I'm gonna die. You gotta come quick, play with your tits baby."

Brooke moaned and lifted her hands to her breasts, pinching each of her nipples and rolling them between her thumb and forefingers. Because she was pregnant she was so sensitive everywhere and it didn't take long for her to explode and fill my tongue with her cum. It was fucking amazing. Slowly I crawled up her body, kissing her as I went until the head of my cock was notched in her opening.

Brooke

The things David did to me had to be wrong, they couldn't be right or good but they felt so damn good I couldn't make him stop. He had the head of his penis just inside the opening of my vagina and I thought he was just going to surge in but I was wrong.

He pushed so slowly and gently until he was finally seated so deep inside me. He stopped and leaned his forehead on my shoulder, panting with the effort of not moving, letting me get used to him filling me so completely.

I started to feel like this wasn't enough, that he needed to move and I raised my knees, widening my hips so he slid in just a little farther. We both moaned at the same time and then David finally started to move.

He pulled back until he was almost completely out of me then slowly pushed back in again. His pace was so slow he was driving me crazy but I didn't know how to make him change it or speed up. I pushed my hips against his but that didn't work. I dug my nails into his back and arched my neck but he just sucked on my throat, making me even crazier.

"David!" I cried, arching my chest against his.

"What Angel, tell me what you want."

"I don't know! More...I don't know."

"You want me to go faster baby?" He asked, matching his movements to his words and causing the spiral to begin. I nodded and bit my lower lip, moaning but still so far from what I really needed. "You want it harder baby?" He asked, slamming his hips into mine.

Yup, there it was . . . I was so close . . . just . . . and then I was clenching my jaw and arching my back and digging my nails into David's shoulders and coming and it was so very amazing.

He pumped into me two, three, four more times then tensed over me and groaned as he let go. He slumped to the side, pulling me against him and burying his nose in my hair.

"Thank you." He said and I giggled. "Come on, let's go have a bath and clean up."

***

The next two months went super-fast. The guys got into Demon's safety deposit box and were going through everything they found there. Michelle got her letter from her dad and so much more of her life with her mom made sense now. She never understood why her mom never moved on with another man but it turned out Demon and Jen were still married and very much in love.

Michelle wondered when she got a little older how her mom could afford to have a house and a car and could buy food and clothes when she didn't work. It was because Demon paid for everything.

In case they had to pick up quickly and leave, Demon didn't want anything to hold them back. Jen didn't work and Demon would come and visit as often as he could when Michelle was in school. He hated not seeing her but he knew it was the best for her safety.

It seemed that Jen was an officer in the same black ops group that Demon was part of. They had met there and fallen in love but they both knew they couldn't just leave CMNSS. They were careful but just not careful enough.

Seether especially was enjoying having all the papers to go through. It meant he didn't have to do any of the physical work on the Ord Road project. Not that he was against physical labour, but it had to be done in warm weather and coming to the end of November, even in Kamloops was cold.

The Ord Road project was going well. The MCs construction company was building four-plexes for the families who needed more space and eight-plexes for the people who only needed one or two rooms.

The club had four main construction teams on their payroll and all of them were working on Ord Road, hoping they would get it done by Christmas. It was a tall order. The city was working with the company to keep permits and paper work up to date and happening fast.

It was Tuesday afternoon and I was walking into the veteran's center for my regular shift, looking for Josh. He wasn't at his usual table but maybe he was just late. I put my things away in my locker then went in search of my boss to find out what I had to do for the day. I was starting to really get excited.

I had felt the baby move for the first time last night and had gotten David all excited but he couldn't feel anything. My ultrasound was tomorrow and we were going to find out what we were having. I thought back to the first time I met David's sister and Hammer.

They had just come over for supper because I hadn't met Kat and Hammer I had only met for a few seconds months ago. Kat was complaining about the still constant morning sickness and I said mine wasn't bothering me at all anymore. Both Kat and Hammer gave me a look like my head had just turned right around then looked at David.

"I hadn't told them." He said sheepishly, rubbing the back of his head.

"Oh," I whispered, looking between David and Kat. She had tears in her eyes and Hammer wrapped his arms around her thinking she was upset. "I'm sorry; I thought David had told you. Um, I'm due in March."

"Oh my God, our kids are going to grow up together!" She exclaimed, jumping up and down and rushing to her brother to hug him. "I'm due in May!"

She had gone and gotten an ultrasound a few days before to see if they could tell how far along she was and they discovered she was having twins. She was freaking out about being pregnant but so excited to be having twins while Hammer was good with the pregnancy but wasn't sure what they would do with two babies.

Now, I walked back into the main room of the center and Josh was still not in his usual spot. I looked around thinking maybe he had decided to change it up a bit. He had been coming to this center for ten years and had sat in the same spot every day for every one of those ten years. Delores my boss walked by and I stopped her with a hand on her arm.

"Delores, do you know where Josh is?"

"Oh dear, you didn't hear? Josh died the other night. He took an entire bottle of sleeping pills and just never woke up." She said, shaking her head. "It was so sad, he had no family left and there isn't anyone to claim his body and give him a funeral. It's horrible really, he served our country as he did and he won't get any recognition. I would pay for his funeral if I could."

"I can." I said, fighting tears. "Delores, I need to go, I'm sorry this isn't right. I know people who can fix this."

"All right dear," Delores said, smiling as I rushed away from her.

I hurried out of the building and drove as fast as I could out to the MCs clubhouse. This wasn't right, Josh needed to be recognized and have a proper burial. I managed to fight my tears until I walked in the front door of the clubhouse. It was still pretty early so no one was really around except for a young man behind the bar.

"Excuse me; I need to find David Bishop."

"Who?"

"Um, Axle? I need to speak to Axle." Just then Logan came out of his office and spotted me talking to this kid, really.

"Brooke, what are you doing here?" Logan asked walking over and placing his hand on my shoulder. "Is everything all right, there's nothing wrong with the baby is there?"

"No, no, the baby is fine, I need to find David. Josh died the other night."

"Josh the Lieutenant who helped us with that code?" I just nodded, feeling my lip start to quiver and tears track down my cheeks. "Come on," he said wrapping an arm around my shoulder and pulling me against him. "Prospect, get Axle in my office yesterday, tell him his Angel is here and she's crying. That'll get his ass moving."

Logan walked me into his office and sat me on the leather couch that was against one wall. He rushed over to the mini fridge behind his desk and brought me a bottle of water and opened it for me. Before either of us could say anything or I could even take a drink David was there busting through the door.

"What's wrong, why the fuck is she crying, what did you do?" He demanded panting.

CHAPTER 12
Axle

"I didn't fucking do anything." Logan snapped indignantly. "She was crying when she got here."

"Angel baby, what's wrong?" I asked, kneeling in front of her and shoving Logan out of the way.

"David stop, Logan has been very nice."

"Lo," we both said at the same time.

"Pardon me?"

"He doesn't like to be called Logan." I explained. "Even Alana calls him Lo."

"Oh, ok."

"Please baby, tell me what's wrong." I pleaded, moving off the floor onto the couch and cupping her wet cheeks in my hands.

"Josh died the other night." she said biting her bottom lip trying to hold back more tears.

"What, how?"

"He took a months-worth of sleeping pills and didn't wake up. David, he had no family to look after him." She said wrapping her fingers around one of my hands.

"The Legion provides for funeral and burial expenses babe." I said softly, smoothing her hair off her face.

"Oh, I thought he was all alone and no one would take care of him." She whispered ducking her head.

"If that had been the case we would have taken care of him." Lo said gently from his desk. "We can still contribute. We all have our uniforms still; we can wear full dress and act as pallbearers. We could have the drums with the graveside processional. Josh's headdress, insignia and medals are borne on a velvet cushion into the service and we can fire over the grave when the body is interred. We have enough guys here who can perform all the different positions included the Last Post, doesn't one of the guys still have his trumpet or bugle or something?"

"Really, you'd do all that for a man you'd never met?" Brooke asked, looking stupefied.

"I would do it for anyone whether I met them or not." Lo said fiercely but kindly. "Whether I served with a man or woman directly they are still my brother or sister and are a part of my family. Every one of us here at the club believes that."

Brooke smiled at Lo and nodded. She seemed to be happy about the outcome of her mad dash out to the clubhouse. Josh would be taken care of and it was the least we could do for him given what he'd done for us.

"You know Lo," I said looking over at him, pulling Brooke under my arm and relaxing back on the couch with her. "We could do something more. I don't know what exactly the Legion does for veterans with limited funds or no money. Do you know if those men and women get the full military burial?"

"No," Lo said, shaking his head. "I don't know what the legion does. We can certainly get Seether on it and offer our services. If there aren't any forces members in the area who are able to participate in a military funeral for the men and women without family then we are more than capable of standing up and being a part of that."

I nodded and hugged Brooke tight; knowing that deep down this is what she wanted. For Josh and others like him to be recognized the way they deserved to be.

The next morning I was standing at the bottom of the stairs yelling up at Brooke to hurry up.

"I can't hurry up! If I move much faster I'm going to pee my pants!" She yelled back, I'm pretty sure I heard her mutter for me to shut up, too.

My girl was getting quite the potty mouth since hanging out with me, I might just get her swearing for real soon.

"If you've gotta pee then go pee." I said, thinking I was being so sensible.

"I can't, I had to drink a litre of water for the ultrasound, I can't pee now." She replied, finally appearing on the stairs.

She looked amazing in nothing more spectacular than jeans and a t-shirt but pregnancy made her already ethereal, angelic look glow.

"What the hell are you talking about?"

"Do you know what an ultrasound is?"

"Only vaguely," I answered completely honestly, shrugging.

"It's sound waves that are shot through the fluid surrounding the baby that bounce back after hitting the baby and that's how we get a picture. A full bladder makes the cervix easier to see to make sure it's completely closed like it's supposed to be."

"This isn't supposed to weird me out is it?"

"No David, you should not be weirded out by this. You're about to see our baby for the first time. Are you still sure you want to find out what we're having?" By this time we were in my truck and on our way to the Interior Health building.

"Yeah I'm sure. I really don't care if we find out Angel. If you want to know then I am happy to know, if you want to wait then I am happy to wait." I said shrugging.

I did want to know, though. I didn't know what I wanted, a boy I could teach stuff to or a girl just like my angel. It was hard to decide.

"Have you thought of any names you like?" Brooke asked looking over at me. I couldn't tell if she was testing me or not.

"Honestly no. Kat said if they have a boy his name will be Alex David after me. Hammer hates his name and doesn't want a junior so Samuel is completely off the table for them. Kat said though if they had a girl her name would be Lexa Judith after me and Hammer's mom. What about your parents? Did they have names you want to pass on or use?"

"Really? My parents had rather odd names, are you sure you would want to use them?"

"I don't know; what were they?"

"You ready for this?" She asked, looking a bit skeptical. I motioned for her to continue and she took a deep breath. "My dad was Wallace Alfred and my mom was Imogen Florence."

"You're right, we can't use those names, although Imogen isn't horrible."

"It's not?" She demanded, shocked that I would say such a thing. I snorted at her and shook my head.

"What about your grandparents, what were their names?"

"Weird but not as weird, you ready?" I nodded at her to continue as we pulled into the parking lot of the health center. Eli Augustine and Antonia Adeline were the grandparents who raised me, and John Arthur and Mary Grace were my dad's parents."

"Huh," I said, parking the truck. I was still thinking about those names when the technician called me to go back and see our baby.

Brooke had been in the back for quite some time and I was starting to get a bit worried.

The first thing Brooke said to me was; "I got to pee."

I snorted and congratulated her on holding it in as long as she did and kissed her lips lightly.

"Well Daddy, are you ready to meet your little person?" The technician asked sitting back at the funny looking computer.

"I guess so." I said smiling at Brooke

"Just a bit more jelly and we'll get started." The technician squirted some slimy stuff on Brooke's little belly and started running a wand through it all over her. The screen flashed and I looked up to see what looked like the head of a baby in profile.

"Is that -?"

"You bet that there is your baby." The technician pointed out different things like the fluttering of the baby's heartbeat and his/her little toes. She outlined the little head with her finger and showed where the baby was sucking it's thumb. I could feel my eyes filling with tears but I couldn't make them stop and I wasn't sure I wanted to.

"Now, moment of truth, do you want to know what you're having?"

"Yes, please," Brooke said looking over at the technician. She had been watching me with a sweet smile on her face the whole time I was seeing our baby. She squeezed my hand and rubbed her thumb over my knuckles.

"Let's see if this little one will behave and let us see what the secret is." The technician waved her wand around and smiled. "Well, this little one is going to keep you both on your toes for sure. I can't legally tell you what you're having but all the information will be at your doctor's office by tomorrow. You can call them and ask them to tell you. Often they write that information on a piece of paper and put it in an envelope and you can pick it up and find out together."

I sighed slightly irritated but I did understand that this wasn't this woman's fault. I smiled at her and shook her hand, thanking her for everything and helped Brooke clean up.

"Your pictures will be at the front desk when you're ready." The technician said as she left the room.

"Pictures?" I said looking at Brooke.

"Yeah, they take pictures of the baby for us to have." She said smiling. I took her hand and we left the room, got our pictures and went to get lunch.

"Why can't the tech tell us what we're having?" I asked, curious.

"Because there are people who will have abortions if the baby isn't the sex they want." She said sadly.

"That's fucking stupid."

She just shrugged but I could see that it bothered her a lot that someone would destroy a life so easily. She called her doctor and explained what she wanted and they agreed that the information would be at the reception desk by the time the clinic closed. We went for lunch but she was quiet and said very little.

"What's the matter Angel?"

"Hmm, oh I don't know. Just thinking of Josh I guess. He had to be so lonely to take his life like that, it's just sad." She shrugged but didn't say anything else for the rest of our meal.

What she said started me thinking, she obviously had a big heart and needed in her soul to do something to help others. I wondered if there was something I could do to help her find that place in her life.

CHAPTER 13

Brooke

The next day I picked up the envelope from my doctor that would tell David and I what our baby was. I was so excited but so sad at the same time. I didn't know Josh well, but I missed his presence and I regretted not getting to know him better.

As I drove to the clubhouse to see David I thought about Josh and his upcoming funeral. Because he had died outside of a hospital and under somewhat suspicious circumstances an autopsy had to be done.

Thankfully the pathologist in Kelowna was able to perform the autopsy and Josh's body didn't need to be sent to Vancouver. The results from the autopsy and tests would be done in less than a week and we could have Josh back to bury him.

I pulled into the clubhouse parking lot and found David and Hammer outside yelling at each other and pushing each other. Lo and Kat were leaning against the front of the clubhouse completely calm, watching the fight in front of them.

"What's going on?" I demanded walking up to Lo and Kat. They both looked over at me completely bored.

"Oh, Sam did something stupid." Kat replied with her arms folded over her chest and resting on her belly. She was bigger than I was but she had two babies inside her while I only had one.

"Oh dear," I said, turning to lean against the building with Kat. "Shouldn't we intervene?"

"Nah, Lo's enjoying the show. They won't hurt each other too badly, it's not like they're really mad and they do still like each other. I mean, they are going to be sort of related soon." Kat shrugged.

"What did Hammer do that made David so angry?"

"Not a clue; Sam might not have actually done anything, for all I know Axle's mad about something else and Sam asked him a totally innocent question and Axle flew off the handle. For all I know he told Axle about the p-spot orgasm I gave him like he did Lo." Kat replied smiling fondly at the two big men pushing and shoving each other while Lo sputtered and laughed.

So far as I could tell there hadn't been any punches thrown but there were a lot of insults being thrown if the noise in front of us was any indication.

"The what?" I demanded, I had no idea what a p-spot orgasm was or why it would embarrass Lo so much to talk about it.

"Ask Axle about it later." Kat replied, bouncing her eyebrows up and down.

"Hammer asked Axle for permission to ask you to marry him." Lo rumbled beside us chuckling.

"What?" Kat screeched turning on her brother's friend then turning back to her brother and apparently soon to be fiancé and rushed over to them. "David!"

I looked over at Lo who was laughing as he watched his friends yelling at each other over Kat's head. They were both easily a foot taller than her and were squishing her between them.

Before she could say anything else David wrapped his arms around her and turned her to face Hammer who was on one knee in front of her with a ring held out. I didn't hear what he said but the diamond on the ring had to be huge because it was glinting in the sunlight.

"Hand it over." Lo said to me just as Kat tackled Hammer to the ground and kissed him.

Just as I turned to Lo to ask him what he meant Seether came out of the building at our backs. I turned to say hi to him and smiled.

"Hey Brooke, he means the envelope with the baby's gender. Alana made him promise to get it before you opened it. Something about a gender reveal party this weekend." Seether said, taking a huge bite out of the sandwich he had brought with him.

"Oh no, no no no no, I am not waiting until this weekend to find out what this baby is. If Alana wants to do a gender reveal party she has two hours to get it together." I said, shaking my head adamantly. I was not waiting any longer than I absolutely had to.

"Done." Lo said, holding his hand out for the envelope. "She's over at the house right now sending me text after text. I've gotten so many messages in the last five minutes since you got here I think my butt's numb." David walked up just as I handed Lo the envelope with a huge smile on his face.

"What's this?" David demanded. "Is that my baby girl?"

"Girl?" I asked, confused, did he know something I didn't?

"Trying it out," he said, shrugging.

"Oh, it very well may be." I said laughing at him. "How does it feel, baby girl?"

"Scary as hell." He replied smiling.

"Well, Alana wants to do a gender reveal party so I had to give Lo the envelope before I even looked in it. Guess we have to wait another couple of hours, but that's better than the week Alana wanted." I said chuckling.

"Nah," Lo said smiling. "She knew you wouldn't wait another

week. When Axle told her you were getting the envelope today she had it all planned last night. Just be at the house by seven." Then he turned and walked away. I watched him go with a small frown on my face.

"Come on," David said looking at his watch. "We've got almost two hours before we have to be over there. I need a shower; join me?"

"Oh, I can just wait for you in your room or the main area." I said nervously. We had been making love just about every night since my cookie baking explosion. I still had batches in the freezer because David said they were best warmed up in the microwave so they were soft and gooey. I'd created a monster.

We hadn't however gone back into the shower together since that night I had surprised him and we had fought about condoms. I wondered if I was missing out on something and I was sure I was but I couldn't make myself go through that again.

I didn't think David would do the same thing, or that we would fight but every time I thought about stepping into the shower with him all I remembered was the pain I felt while I slumped on the floor of my room, naked and alone.

"No Angel baby, I want you to shower with me." He whispered then licked the shell of my ear. "Let me make the sad memories better. I fucked it up last time, let me fix it."

I looked up at him and nodded, letting him take my hand and lead me into the clubhouse and his room. I had been here before but that was almost six months ago. Nothing had changed in that time, though but his TV was noticeably missing.

David pulled his shirt over his head then wrapped his arms around me and kissed me sweetly, sipping from my lips until I'd had enough of the teasing and I grabbed handfuls of his hair and made him kiss me properly.

He smiled against my mouth then chuckled. He ran his hands up my sides under my shirt and his rough hands left a trail of fire right to the clasp at the back of my bra. Before I knew what he was doing my shirt and bra were gone and he was bent and sucking on my nipples.

Oh God, my very sensitive nipples. They were so sensitive right now David was just about able to get me to orgasm just licking and sucking on them. He kissed up my chest again, stopping every couple of inches to suck on my neck and then my jaw before he reached my mouth and kissed me deeply again.

"Get naked Angel, I'm gonna go start the shower." He was panting and his jeans were bulging from his erection.

Before he could turn and walk away I smiled and grabbed the waistband of his jeans, pulling on the snap and slipping the zipper down as I pushed my hand into his underwear to cup him. I stroked him a few times pulling on his nipple ring with my other hand. It didn't take long before he stopped me with a hand tight around my wrist.

"Baby stop, you keep that up and I'm not gonna last long enough to get inside you."

He kissed me hard again then walked away, "Get naked, you've got two minutes, the water heats up fast."

He shot over his shoulder. I didn't have to be told more than twice, I toed off my shoes and shoved my maternity pants down my legs but in my haste they got stuck around my feet.

"You're two minutes . . . Oh fuck baby! You should always be naked and bent over when I come into the room." David said quickly walking over to cup my bottom. "Put your hands on the bed baby."

"David, I'm stuck." I whimpered.

"That's just fine, I've been wanting to taste you like this." He whispered then licked from my clit up to my asshole.

"David!" I shrieked trying to move away from him when he swirled his tongue around my anus.

"Don't worry Angel baby, I'm not going in there, just had to have a taste." He did it again and I couldn't keep myself from groaning. Anal sex was wrong in the eyes of the church and I didn't want that but having him play back there felt amazing. "Your skin tastes like heaven." He whispered, his voice rumbling against my sensitive skin.

I whimpered again as he lifted my legs so I was kneeling on the bed then pulled my pants and socks off my feet. He ran his warm calloused hands up my legs, massaging my ass cheeks then grasping me around the waist, lifting me off the bed.

"Come on Angel let's get you in the shower." He turned me to face him and lifted me, my legs automatically wrapping around his waist. He had taken his jeans and underwear off in the bathroom so his hard cock nudged up between my legs and every step he took rubbed him against me deliciously.

One of his arms was holding me under my ass and the other hand pulled the shower curtain open and then closed. The whole time I was kissing him, sucking and nipping at his jaw until he slowly put me down so my feet just touched the floor of the shower.

He kissed me again, his mouth taking complete command of mine all the while pushing me against the cold tile wall. He left my mouth and I whimpered as he kissed a hot trail down between and underneath my breasts then down to my belly button and licked inside. I knew where he was going but he was taking so long I was going crazy.

"David," I begged, trying to hurry him but it seemed to have the opposite effect. Slowly he trailed his tongue under the small swell of my belly then sucked on my hip bone, nipping the skin there gently. "Please David … "

I tried to squeeze my thighs together to relieve the ache there but he just chuckled and forced my legs apart. With his fingers he parted the lips of my pussy and gently played with the sensitive flesh there. Before I knew what he was doing he had turned me to face the wall and he was sitting below me with his back against the wall.

"Brace your hands on the wall Angel." He rasped, burying his nose between my legs and taking a deep breath. "I'm gonna be down here a long while."

CHAPTER 14

Axle

The second I latched my mouth onto her clit and swirled my tongue around her pussy she screamed, throwing her head back. She was so sensitive because of her pregnancy that it didn't take me long to make her cum but then she was sore so I had to be quick.

I swiveled a finger in her dripping pussy, gathering her wetness and spreading it over her ass hole, lubricating it for my finger. I knew she wasn't ready for actual anal penetration and would probably never be, and that was fine with me but I wanted her to feel how amazing just a little penetration could be between lovers.

"David?" She cried, looking down at me with wide eyes.

I didn't answer her, just looking up at her as I sucked her clit deeper into my mouth, flicking it with my tongue and pushing my finger a little farther into her ass. It took maybe a second before she was moaning and throwing her head back again.

"Lock your knees Angel." I whispered when her thighs started to shake with the force of her coming orgasm.

She did as I told her to and pushed back against my finger in her ass. She panted above me then screamed when I pumped two fingers into her pussy, crooking them and rubbing her g-spot. I pumped a few times; easing her through the orgasm then took one hand from her and grasped her hip.

"Bend your knees, come down to me, I'll catch you Angel."

She slid down until her pussy was poised just above my rock hard cock and I guided her to sink onto it. As I slid into her tight seethe I left my finger in her ass, knowing it would make her feel even more full.

Then I bent my knees and braced my feet against the other side of the tub, cradling her within my limbs and began pumping up into her laying her back against my legs.

Her hair cascaded down my lower legs as she arched her neck back and pushed her breasts high into the air as she orgasmed again, this time so hard her inner muscles milked my cock and I thought I was going to lose circulation.

When she came back down I gently pulled my finger from her and gripped her hips in both hands and pumped up into her hard.

Brooke curled up against me and braced her hands on my shoulders, holding on tight. Her new position gave me an idea and I quickly pulled her off me and turned her around on my lap. I placed her hands on the edge of the tub and slammed into her again from behind.

David!" She shrieked looking at me over her shoulder, her eyes dark with desire.

"Come again Brooke," I commanded, pumping into her furiously.

"I can't..." She wailed but I could tell she really wanted to. It was building in her again and damn if I was going to leave her hanging.

I reached around and pinched her clit and she exploded again, losing her grip on the tub and falling against my legs. Feeling her grip my dick as hard as she was made me cum and I let go and filled her with it.

We sat there panting like that for a few minutes before Brooke finally roused enough to turn her head and look at me.

"What's a p-spot orgasm?"

"What," that was not what I was expecting to come out of her mouth.

"Kat and Lo were talking about it earlier while you were play fighting with Hammer."

"Woah, stop, you're talking about sexual things and my baby sister in the same sentence. I don't want to know any of that."

"Ok," Brooke said, giggling and leaning back against my chest. "What is it then?"

"You know where I had my finger?" I asked her, brushing her hair off her neck so I could suck and nibble there.

"Mmm-hmmm," she murmured, tipping her head to the side.

"Well if you were to do that to me and rub my prostate I would cum like a fucking elephant." I said nipping her ear lobe.

"Oh," she jumped a bit at the bite then settled as I soothed it. "Do you want that?"

"Doesn't matter to me, if you wanted to do it I wouldn't say no but if you don't want to I won't ask for it." I said, patting her butt. "Come on Angel, Alana's gonna be expecting us soon and I got another position I wanna show you here in the shower."

Brooke

I was coming to realize that David was completely insatiable. He had soothed my sore flesh with his hands and washed me until I was dying to have him inside me again. Then he lifted me up and wrapped my legs around his waist and fucked me hard against the wall, his word.

I would never in a million years use that word to describe the act of making love but I was coming to understand that when David said it he wasn't demeaning the act or making it dirty, just using a different word.

We stepped into Alana's house and everything looked exactly like it always did. This definitely did not look like a usual Alana party. There were no streamers or balloons and nothing was decorated at all. There was no music, or food or people.

Except for Lo sitting in the arm chair he had bought for the house when Alana and the kids had moved in. They still weren't living together because Alana thought that set a bad example for the kids, so Lo had moved them into the ranch house on the club's property. He was here as often as he was at the clubhouse and this was much more convenient for the club than for him to be at her condo all the time.

"Where is everybody?" David asked Lo, expecting like me that there would be tons of people around. Lo just looked up at us and smiled and then thirty people jumped out of various places around the house yelling surprise and tossing pink balloons.

"Pink?" I exclaimed. "Does that mean what I think it does?"

"What does pink mean?" Joann, Alana's mother asked.

"So, only four of us here knew this was a gender reveal party." Alana said, smiling at everyone in the room. "So pink balloons are yes for your baby girl." She said bouncing on her toes and clapping her hands together.

I looked up at David with my fingers over my lips and smiled, tears in my eyes.

"We're having a girl!" I exclaimed then threw my arms out and wrapped them around his neck. Then I stopped and thought about the expression I just saw on his face. There wasn't one and I pulled back worried to look at him. "Are you ok?"

"Yeah," he whispered, letting his own tears track down his face then he squeezed me tight and buried his face in my throat. "Imogen Adeline." He knelt in front of me and kissed my belly, rubbing his thumbs over our baby. "It's so nice to meet you Imogen Adeline." He placed his cheek against our baby and took a deep breath, holding me tight around my hips.

"Holy fuck! It looks like a bottle of pepto bismol blew up in here." Lo said from his chair, making us all laugh. "Come on daddy, let's get you a beer."

David got up from his knees and kissed me lightly on the lips then followed Lo into the kitchen. I was wrong, there was food everywhere, it was just hiding with all the people. Which was a really good thing since David had worked up a huge appetite.

"Imogen Adeline?" Alana asked, nudging me with her hip. "Where did that come from?"

"My mom and one of my grandma's," I said smiling at her and biting into something that tasted like heaven. "What is this?"

"I'm surprised you're eating that, it's avocado, you hate avocado." She replied, her eyes wide.

"Has it always tasted this good and I never knew?" I demanded thinking I had been missing out on something all this time.

"It's always tasted the same, whether it tasted that good I don't know. Pregnancy can change your taste buds."

"Oh," I pouted. "Does that mean that I'm going to hate it again once the baby is born?"

"Maybe," Alana laughed and shrugged, "but maybe not."

"I guess we'll have to wait four more months to find out, eh?" I smiled at her as David wrapped his arm around my waist.

"Wait for what?" He asked looking down at us.

"To see if I'll still like avocado after I have the baby." I replied smiling up at him.

"You hate avocado." He shot back wrinkling his nose.

"Apparently Imogen loves it." I laughed, popping another piece of the cracker with avocado and something else I didn't care about into my mouth. David smiled at me indulgently and hugged me tight.

"Imogen," he whispered lifting his beer bottle to his lips, "I fucking love it."

CHAPTER 15

Brooke

It was a week later and we were getting ready for Josh's funeral. David, Lo, Hammer, Seether, Tank, and Sharpie had been asked to act as pallbearers for Josh's casket. It was strange to think that Josh's casket was shorter than most because of his missing legs and would need six pallbearers instead of the usual eight. What a weird thought.

Besides the six guys, almost the entire club would be in attendance in their dress uniforms. Three of the prospects would perform the gun salute but only three shots would be fired, David said the 21 gun salute was an American tradition and often Canadian military funerals didn't have guns fired at all but Butch, the clubs accountant would play the Last Post on his trumpet. The club had also hired a bagpipe player to play after Butch and after the casket was interred.

David was in our room now putting the finishing touches on his uniform and polishing his boots before putting them on. He was so handsome anyway, but in his dress uniform, with his face shaved and his hair cut short he was extraordinary.

His chest was full of medals and last night when he'd pulled his uniform out of the closet to hang it and press it I'd asked what they all meant.

"They mean a lot of things." He said touching each reverently. "The green, red, white and blue is a Peacekeeping Service Medal. The red, black and gold is for Champion Shot. The red and white bars are Canadian Forces Decoration, there is a Medal of Military Valor, Meritorious Service Cross and Special Service Medal. The two blue and white ones are for NATO, the first one for serving in Kosovo and the second for assisting with the American military after 9/11."

"I am so sorry for what you had to go through to get these." I whispered. He took a deep breath through his nose and let it go slowly bringing himself back under control.

"Me too," He said, kissing the top of my head.

"If this is too hard you don't have to do it." I said, hoping I was being understanding.

"It's because this is so hard that I have to do this." He replied kissing me.

Now, I touched his shoulder as he sat on the bed tying his laces. He looked up and kissed my belly then stood in front of me. I reached up and straightened his collar. His uniform was a simple but elegant navy single breasted jacket with a mandarin collar. His rank was clear on his uniform and his medals and ribbons stood out proudly on his chest.

He reached down and took his tan beret off the dresser and tucked it under his arm.

"You look so smart," I said, cupping his smooth cheek in my hand. "And sad."

He smirked and sighed. "Yeah, I didn't get to know Josh enough. Maybe if I had made more of an effort he wouldn't have swallowed those pills."

"You can't think that." I said shaking my head in denial. Josh had indeed died of a self-induced overdose of sleeping pills. "It's heartbreaking to think we could have or should have done more, but how could we know? God gave us free will and Josh exercised his, blaming ourselves for Josh's choice is changing the meaning of that choice. We need to look instead at how we can change the mind of someone who's still alive and contemplating the same thing."

He kissed me on the lips and we left for the Cemetery. Because we didn't know what religion Josh followed or any at all we agreed with the funeral home and the Royal Canadian Legion that we would have a quick service at the grave site.

I asked one of the priests from the church to come and speak about grief and death and mourning and whatever he thought appropriate and to bless the body as it was interred.

The thirty members of the MC who were able to make it to the service were in their uniforms and as the casket was carried by the six guys to the grave site the three prospects performed the silent gun salute and Father James spoke very clearly and even comfortingly about Josh and the sacrifices our men and women in the forces make. Many of the women present had tears in our eyes but the men in uniform stood stoically.

When the casket was lowered, Butch played the Last Post and all those in uniform stood at attention and saluted Josh one last time, then as we all turned to leave the bag pipes started to play and I couldn't move my feet.

I was rooted to the ground, heaving deep sobs. David stepped in front of me and wrapped me in his arms, holding me to his chest and burying his face in my neck. I could feel his tears as we held each other and shared our despair.

When our tears finally subsided David squeezed me once again then pulled back to look into my eyes.

"I've been thinking a lot these past few months." He said seriously.

"Oh, should I be worried?"

"No," he chuckled, "I don't think so. First, do you want to go back to teaching?"

"I don't know," I said shrugging one shoulder, "I hadn't really thought that much about it." Which was true, I missed teaching and I missed the kids but I didn't feel like my life was over because I didn't have that.

"Well you have a degree in education right?"

"I have two degrees, one in early childhood education and the second in psychology." I corrected him, wondering what exactly he was getting at.

"Why don't you get your Masters in Clinical Psychology and then you could counsel. You could choose to counsel people like Josh and you could work out of the center if that's what they wanted, or you could work out of the clubhouse. That's the whole reason Lo and I started this club."

He was explaining something I should have asked him about long ago but had been so caught up in my own drama.

"We left the forces feeling adrift, like we didn't belong anywhere and weren't completely welcomed anywhere. We needed that tight bond we had when we were active and we knew we weren't the only guys and girls missing it. We knew a lot of our friends from overseas were committing suicide and were depressed and we knew there was a lot more we could be doing.

"We came here, started the club and opened it up to any non-active duty member of the forces regardless of age, sex or rank. We set it up like an MC but only because we liked motorcycles and fixing bikes was a good profession to put guys in once they were a little more integrated, that and the horses. Anyway, we don't have an in-house counselor, but maybe you want to do it."

I blinked up at him for a few seconds, shocked by all that he had said, "Wow, you have been thinking about this. Have you talked to Lo about having an in-house counselor?"

"No, like I said, just thinking but we had sort of talked about it a while ago. We have a regular therapist that our guys see but she's not on the premises." I nodded, still staring up at him. "You're making me a little uncomfortable."

"Sorry," I said smiling. "Let's go talk to Lo."

"What?" He demanded as I walked away.

"I like your idea, but doesn't this all depend on what Lo thinks? Let's go talk to Lo."

CHAPTER 16

Axle

When Brooke and I got to the clubhouse most of the guys who were at the funeral were sitting around the main room, their uniform jackets unbuttoned and beers in front of them. We sat with Lo, Alana, Hammer and Kat and Seether sat down once we were settled.

"Lo, remember a while we talked about in-house counselor or therapist?" I asked without wasting any time.

"Yeah man, you got someone in mind?"

"Brooke." I said holding Lo's gaze with mine to show him how serious I was.

"Brooke, you have a licence or something?" Lo said not looking away from me.

"Uh, not yet Lo but I only have to get my Masters and I can offer counselling. If you wanted me to work with you guys I could concentrate on PTSD sufferers and military veterans." She said, her eyes big and looking around at everyone sitting with us.

Lo sat staring at me for a few minutes, the silence around the table getting denser. Then suddenly he smiled and I knew he saw something I wasn't sure I meant to show him.

"Do it, if that's what you want. We would really like to have an in-house therapist and I think you would be a good fit for that. I was thinking once Ord Road was done we would buy that land on the other side of the ranch house and build a rehab center and barracks. We could build you guys a house out here, too and Brooke you could have an office in the center." He nodded to himself like he was hearing a really good idea. "Find the program you want and let me know, the club will pay for a portion of it."

"What?" Brooke exclaimed, but I just sat back knowing this was what Lo was going to do if he agreed to my idea. The club had lots of money; we could easily afford to pay for each of us to get a Masters degree.

"Sounds good man, it's gotta be something she can do from home 'cause I'm not letting her out of my sight." I said grabbing her hand and squeezing it to calm her.

"This is crazy." She said to Alana who just shrugged. Just then Lo's phone rang and he pulled it out and looked at the screen. He frowned when he didn't recognize the number but answered anyway.

"Yeah?" he said listening. "What the fuck are you talking about?" I snapped my fingers at him trying to get him to put the phone on speaker. He looked at me and nodded.

"That's right," the voice on the other end said, "put me on speaker so all your little minions can hear me."

"What the fuck?" Seether demanded.

"That's right Aiden, I can see into your little clubhouse. Is there a code word to get in?"

"We don't have any cameras in here, how can you see what we're doing? You hiding in the closet?" Lo demanded looking to Seether to explain. He just shrugged and shook his head.

"Are you sure about that? There are no cameras that you know of or can see, that doesn't mean there aren't any cameras. Let's get down to business. I want you shit heads out of my town."

"Fuck no." I breathed shaking my head.

"Fuck yes David, or is it Axle? It's hard to remember when the Angel baby calls you David but everyone else calls you Axle. Hi Brooke, how you doin' sweetie, pregnancy treating you ok? Here's the thing, before you ass holes showed up I had the corner on the market, now you're here and you're infringing on my territory."

"How can we infringe on your territory when we don't engage in the same business as you do. In fact we don't deal in any illegal businesses so why do you think getting us out of town will help you?"

"Briggs," was the only answer.

"Briggs fed you a load of lies," I said leaning forward a little. I was super tense and angry since I had heard this douche call Brooke Angel baby. I only called her that when we were alone and intimate, which means he bugged her house. "He told us so himself."

"I know, I heard it but that doesn't matter. With a punch like Hammer's I'm sure even the Pope would admit to wrongdoing. Get out of town or I'll bury you all, dead or alive. Alana you think that little deaf kid of yours will see me coming?" She jumped up so fast her chair flew behind her but the voice just laughed and then the call disconnected.

"Lo," She whimpered, turning to him the fear evident on her face.

"I know baby," He said standing and taking her in his arms. "I'll take care of it. You and the boys are safe, I swear it." He held her tight while she trembled then whispered something in her ear and patted her butt. She nodded then left, presumably to go home to the boys. "Meeting now."

"Go to our room, baby," I said, kissing Brooke's cheek. "We're going to stay here tonight and every night until I figure out how that ass wipe got listening devices into our house."

"He got them in here, too didn't he?" She asked worriedly.

"No, Seether has an interference program set up in the clubhouse so outside sources can't get sound. Video apparently yes, but not sound. If that guy heard about anything from Briggs he heard it from the cops, not us." I assured Brooke, rubbing her back. She nodded and kissed my cheek then went quickly to our room. Kat followed her and caught up to her before she disappeared into the hallway.

When the girls were gone we all followed Lo into his office. He sat in his chair and pulled it close to his desk then shoved it back again and started pacing. I had never seen Lo this agitated and I knew the treat against Alana's youngest boy was at the route of it. Before we knew it he had turned and plowed his fist into the drywall behind his desk and pulled back with bloody knuckles.

"Feel better?" Seether asked like the idiot he was.

"Fuck you," Was the answer he got from Lo, Hammer and me but Lo's was most vehement. "He threatened our kids, our women, I do not fucking feel better Aiden!" Lo roared at him, "I will not fucking feel better until this piece of shit is in the ground!"

"Understood Prez," Seether said nodding apologetically. "The program is still working and there haven't been any issues with it but I will go over the readings for the last few months again just to be sure. I did find some very interesting things in all of Demon's notes and papers from the bank, but besides the name of the dealer that I gave you when I first found it and the notes on that case that we forwarded to the cops, there was nothing but the stuff on CMNSS."

"Right, so this dealer, Little D as he calls himself–"

"Douche name." Hammer muttered grimacing.

"So, Little Douche is trying to get us out of town. We need to find this little fuck and put him down. I want him as gone as we can get him without actually killing him ourselves." We all chuckled at the name Lo gave the fucker then got serious.

"We need to find him." I said somberly.

"Yeah, but he could be calling from anywhere. Just because he could see in here doesn't mean he was here; or even right across the street. With technology the way it is these days he could be on the island or in Whitehorse." Seether sighed, tapping his fingers on his leg.

"Is this guy smart enough to pull all this off do you think?" I asked thoughtfully.

"What are you saying Ax?" Lo looked at me curiously.

"I'm just thinking, is this guy smart enough to figure out all this tech shit. We're all pretty fucking smart right? But only Seether is smart enough to mess with all that mess of computers and jammers and shit. After that conversation on the phone is Little Douche that smart?"

"You think he's working with someone?" Hammer asked, frowning.

"I don't know," I said, shrugging, not really sure if that's what I was saying or not. "He was working with Briggs first, and Briggs pretty much used him and dumped him. Douche wasn't even on our radar until Briggs brought him to us through Demon."

"It's definitely something to look into." Lo said nodding. Our meeting continued well into the night as we made plans for Little Douche and whatever he thought he had planned for us.

Brooke

"Brooke," I turned when I heard my name and found Kat trying to hurry after me. I took pity on her since she was so much bigger than me and not as far a long and waited until she caught up. "Let's go to the kitchen first and talk, have a cup of tea."

"Sure," I agreed, smiling a little but still apprehensive about that phone call.

I turned and watched as all the guys went into Lo's office then followed Kat behind the bar. She chatted about nonsense things as she made our tea and boiled the water in the kettle and then sat across the table from me.

"Do you love my brother?"

"What? Wow, you don't pull punches, eh?" I said, chuckling nervously.

"No, I don't pull punches. I love my brother; I want to make sure he's happy. He looks happy, and you look happy and he looks at you with so much love in his eyes and I think he loves you but I want to know about you."

"Oh, well, I..."

Wait, I want to try something. You know how people say a word and you say the first thing that comes to mind? We're going to do that, you can't think about it, just spit it out ok?" I nodded thinking Kat was silly but I agreed to do it anyway.

"Baby," she began.

"Girl," I responded.

"Club."

"Motorbike."

"Cookies."

"Sex."

"David."

"Love."

"Okay, the cookie thing was weird but I got my answer." She said chuckling. "I say cookies and you say sex?"

"Long story." I replied blushing.

"No no, you gotta tell me now." She insisted, "You can't leave me hanging like that."

"The first time David and I made love after we got back together he came home and my kitchen was covered in fresh baked cookies. I'd had a craving and went a little crazy. I still have some in the freezer." I said chuckling.

We laughed over that and she told me about Lo walking in on her while she was researching the p-spot orgasm thing and I swear I peed my pants, I was laughing so hard. Then I asked her about that and how it was and she said she enjoyed doing it for Hammer and he seemed to appreciate it but neither of them wanted to do it all the time.

"I asked David about it when you first mentioned it last week and he freaked out that I used a sexual term in the same sentence as his sister." We snorted and laughed and she played with her ring.

"Does he want you to do it?"

I shrugged, "I asked him that and he said if I wanted to he wouldn't say no but he wasn't asking for it. I get the impression that the feeling at the time is amazing but it's not something anyone wants to talk about."

"Yeah, I'd have to agree with that." Kat said laughing. "So, next weekend is the first of December, do you know what you're going to get Axle?"

"God no! I haven't got a clue what he would like. What about you? Do you know what you're going to get Hammer?"

"Oh yes. Don't say a word - to anyone. We had my ultrasound last week right? Well the tech says to me 'there's baby A, and baby B, and baby C' and I kind of freaked out a little. Sam is already freaked out that we're having twins so I asked the tech not to tell him about the third baby. She agreed but I can't very well keep it from him so I asked for a picture with arrows pointing out each baby. I'm going to frame it and give it to him."

"Well, that explains a lot."

"Yeah, like why I'm so freakin' huge!! I went to the doctor the next day for my regular appointment and she said they would probably have to do a c-section because there were three babies and I'm not exactly a big person. She said though that we could wait until the last minute and see how it goes. Sections in general are not fun, but emergency ones are worse ... or so I've been told."

"How are things with your mom?" I knew she was living in the clubhouse and had started working but I hadn't seen her around much.

"Um ... they're things. It's difficult but she's trying and I'm not not trying so I guess we just see how things go. She's really excited about the babies and is keeping her distance from Axle which is good until he's ready to talk to her."

"He never talks about her." I said shrugging. "I guess it's easy for him to avoid her when he's living at my house, eh?" Kat and I chatted for a few more minutes then both started yawning and decided it was bedtime. We hugged then went into our own rooms.

CHAPTER 17

Brooke

The next week seemed to drag on and it was making me anxious. We had moved mine and David's things back to the clubhouse and had found my cat and brought him with us. I haven't seen the beast in the week we'd been here but his dish was empty at least once a day so he was around somewhere.

I went in to work at the center every day but it just didn't feel the same without Josh. He wasn't loud or very gregarious but his presence we definitely missed. I also got signed up for masters courses through Trinity Western University out of Langley and was set to start distance learning in January. I was lucky, I just sneaked in.

My major problem though that was keeping me awake at night was Kat's question about what I was going to get David for Christmas. What did one get a big bad ass biker?

Finally by Thursday when I was exhausted and David was starting to notice that I wasn't sleeping and I certainly couldn't tell him why I wasn't sleeping, I went to Lo to ask his advice.

"I need your help." I said closing the door of his office. He looked up at me very surprised then the look in his eyes turned very suspicious.

"This doesn't have anything to do with that p-spot shit does it?" He demanded.

"What, no! Why would I ask you about giving David orgasms?"

"This whole thing started when I accidently walked in on Kat researching the whole thing, she's dyslexic so she couldn't just read about it, then she did it and blew Hammer's mind, among other things and then he had to tell me what she was doing 'cause she thought I thought she was actually watching porn. Really it had all flown out of my head long before I even closed the door on Kat and her computer. So please, please tell me you are not here about anything even closely regarding that."

"Oh goodness, no definitely nothing like that. I just don't know what to get David for Christmas." I said quickly, trying to put Lo at ease. He was definitely the last person I would go to for advice on giving David orgasms.

"You mean besides staying with him and loving him and giving him that baby?"

"Yeah, besides all that," I replied, tipping my head to the side quizzically. "I looked on that oddity mall website but I didn't see anything there that was really David. Some cute things that maybe I would put in his stocking or something but nothing that screams Christmas gift from the woman who's having your baby."

I slumped dejected into a chair in front of Lo's desk. I had contemplated his couch for the slumping but it was becoming too hard to get out of the couch.

Lo chuckled at me but shook his head, "You could get him a new jacket, the one he's got is getting a little worn and you could get your name and the baby's name on a patch to put on it. Or you could get him a new bike. I mean, he loves his bike but we all love new toys, but if you want to get Axle a new bike you'll have to commit to $1000+ monthly payments for a few years."

"Oh hell, really? Motorbikes are that expensive?"

"A bike worth having is, yeah. Try kijiji or Craig's list or whatever that is, you might find something there." Lo shrugged apologetically. "Sorry I couldn't be more help."

"No, that's ok. You gave me a couple good ideas. Especially that patch one, I think David really likes his current jacket but I might get him a couple of patches."

I thanked Lo and left his office going straight to David's room. He always said it was our room but it wasn't, not really. He had it before he met me and even though he hadn't slept with any one for a long time before me he still brought women here.

Not that it mattered; we only slept here for the time being because of Little D. The guys had another name for him but I just couldn't bring myself to say it.

I sat on David's bed and pulled up kijiji on my laptop, hoping to get some inspiration. I was online for close to an hour before I finally found something that was interesting. In the town just south of us was a military base.

It was the British Columbia Dragoons, 39 CBG Reserve Unit. The BCD is a Primary Reserve unit of the Canadian Armed Forces, it's an Armoured Reconnaissance Regiment based in the Okanagan Valley. This coming weekend when I was planning on shopping with Kat there was a sale on old military motorcycles.

It sounded perfect and I could make Kat the mechanic look at whatever I thought about buying.

***

"I cannot believe you convinced me to drive to Vernon in December." Alana bitched from the driver's seat.

"We needed your SUV." Kat said calmly. "I couldn't borrow Sam's 'cause he'd want to ask questions we didn't want to answer, same with Axle, and Judy was working or we'd make her come with us."

"What do you mean she was working? It's Saturday, she works for the school board, the office is closed Saturday!" Alana reasoned.

"She has some new job or something that she's doing part time for a little extra money. I told her if she needed money all she had to do was ask, either Sam or I would give it to her but she said she wanted to do it on her own and wouldn't hear another word about it."

"She's so funny." I said from the back seat. Since getting pregnant Kat started getting car sick if she was in the back seat and I really didn't care where I sat. The drive to Vernon was only just over an hour so it's not like we would be in the car long.

After stopping to pee about ten times though it did take close to two hours. We did finally pull up to a house on the outskirts of town with a huge barn in the back. It was pretty run down and I was starting to wonder if this was the right place and if it was if this was a good idea.

Before I could suggest that we should turn around and I would keep looking, an older man came out of the house, too late to turn back now.

"I'll talk to him, you guys can stay here." I said opening my door.

"No way!" Kat cried, "The whole reason I'm here is because you need a mechanic to make sure you don't get ripped off! I'm coming with you."

"Plus, you're both pregnant, if that guy's gonna cut chunks off you and feed you to his pigs someone's gotta protect you." Alana said, also getting out of the vehicle.

"Can I help you ladies?" The old fellow said from his front porch.

"Hi, I saw online that you had some older model motorcycles for sale? I was wondering if we could look at them and possibly purchase one?" I asked nervously.

"Oh, that son of mine posted that ad again did he?" the old man laughed. "He's always trying to get me to clean out my barn.

Name's William, call me Bill, I'll get my coat and take you out to take a look."

He ducked back into the house and we looked at each other hopefully. Bill came back out and we slowly moseyed out to the dilapidated barn.

"Is that safe?" Alana asked looking pointedly at the barn.

"Probably not," Bill snorted, "Which is probably why my son is trying to get me to sell all my bikes, doesn't want me in here when it all falls down."

He cackled at his joke then motioned us forward to look at his collection. There were bikes of every shape and size, some Harleys, some Norton's some I had never even heard of.

"Are any of them for sale?" I asked, looking around me.

"Well, for the right price just about anything is for sale." Bill said, shrugging his frail shoulders.

"Are there any that need a lot of work?"

"Don't you want one that's in really good shape for Axle to ride?" Alana asked, looking at me strangely.

"No, he has a bike he can ride. I want to get him a bike he can work on and make his own but that has a shared history with him. If I just wanted to buy him a nice bike I'd go to the Harley store at home." I said shaking my head.

Kat was engrossed in one of the bikes down the row and when I looked over at her something else caught my eye. I walked over to it and stood staring at the perfect gift for David.

It was a mess. I don't think it even ran but it was exactly what I was looking for without me even knowing it. Kat walked over and stood beside me looking at the bike leaning against the wall of the barn.

"Harley Davidson WLC," She said, shaking her head. "This was beautiful once."

"Could David fix it, get it running?" I asked her, knowing she would know if her brother would be able to do it.

"Oh yeah, he might have to replace a part or two but if anyone could get a bike running it's Axle." She said assuredly.

"Is this bike for sale?" I asked Bill, turning towards him. He ambled slowly over to us and looked at wreckage.

"You know, in fair condition, that bike is worth about $10,000." He said thoughtfully, scratching at the scruff on his cheeks.

"Yes well, this particular bike is in far from fair condition." I retorted.

"True . . . true. I guess I could sell it to you for $5000."

I snorted, I didn't know anything about bikes and by the way Kat was gently nudging me she thought this was a pretty good deal.

"I'll give you $1000 for it." I said crossing my arms over my chest.

"You've got to be kidding." Bill said incredulously.

"Bill, did you serve in the military?" I asked, hoping to play on his conscience.

"Nope." Shit, there went that plan out the window, oh well; in for a penny in for a pound right?

"Well Bill, my fiancé was in the military, as were the men these women with me are involved with. David, my fiancé and Logan, Alana's fiancé, started a motorcycle club and David's sister Kat here is about to marry another one of their members. All the members of their club are former soldiers. All of the men in the club gave exemplary service and I want to get my fiancé a Christmas gift that reflects how much I respect and love him for all he did while he served and all he's done since.

"I want to give him this motorcycle, Bill and I'm going to give it to him but I'm only going to pay you $1000 for it, in cash right here right now."

"Well missy," Bill said, scratching his ear. I was starting to get the feeling Bill needed a bath with all the scratching he was doing but I wasn't about to say that out loud. "I suppose since you put it like that . . . I'll even have it delivered for you and throw in the new seat I got for it a few years ago but got too old to fix it up."

"Thank you Bill." I exclaimed with a huge smile on my face. Our trip had been a success and Alana could stuff it.

CHAPTER 18

Axle

Dammit, Christmas Eve came far too damn fast! Not that I wasn't ready, I've had Brooke's gift for over a month now. I hope she was ready because I couldn't wait any longer. I had gotten Brooke an engagement ring.

I know it seemed kind of fast, we had only met at the end of June and it was just the end of December but I didn't care. I loved her and I was pretty sure she loved me. I told her I would wait for her and I will, but I wanted her to wear my ring while I did the waiting.

Hammer had asked me to help him when he asked Kat to marry him and I was happy to do it. I didn't have anything like that planned for Brooke though. I was just going to ask her at midnight tonight while we were alone in our room. We agreed to share one gift with each other the night before Christmas and do all the rest with Alana and Lo and their family at their house.

Kat and Hammer would be there with Judy and mine and Kat's mom had been invited. I had gotten her a gift that I thought she might like, but it really had been years since I knew what she liked. I hope she liked the seasons pass tickets to the local theatre but if she didn't I wasn't going to lose sleep over it.

Since Christmas Eve was on a Sunday this year Brooke and I decided to have a movie marathon and spend most of the day in bed. We did go to mass early this morning but decided against the midnight mass because she'd been so tired lately. We would go in the morning with Alana's family and Lo then come home and open gifts. We were just finishing our third movie when Brooke suddenly cried out.

"What's the matter?" I asked, concerned.

"Nothing, your daughter just kicked me really hard." She said chuckling, "Come here; see if she'll do it again." Brooke had said that Imogen had been moving a lot lately but never when I was around to feel it.

"You know she'll just stop as soon as I touch you." I pouted.

"Oh stop, come on she just did it again." Brooke took my hand and put it over her belly where she'd last felt our baby kick her.

It took a second but finally Imogen didn't just kick, she pushed against my hand hard and I could actually cup her little foot in my hand.

"Holy shit!" I exclaimed looking down at Brooke's belly then up into her face. She was laughing at me then she grabbed my other hand and put it over her belly on the other side and a little hand pushed against my hand there, too.

"She's stretching," Brooke laughed then grimaced. "Damn that hurts!"

"Really, is there something I can do?" I asked, hating that she was in pain.

"Make March come faster?" She said then shook her head. "Nothing you can do, she's just getting too big for her home is all. It's a good thing, just makes mama uncomfortable."

"Are you sure Angel mama? I hate when you're not feeling good."

"I'm sure." She cupped my cheek and kissed my lips then gasped as Imogen pushed against my hands again. I ducked down and kissed Brooke's belly and laid my cheek against her feeling her pulse.

"Thanks for my gift baby girl." I whispered to my baby. Brooke feathered her fingers through my hair and laughed.

"I have a gift for you," She said, "Well part of it. You can't see the rest until tomorrow and I don't think I can wait until midnight to give it to you."

"You realize midnight is only six hours away right?" I asked her skeptically.

"I know, but it took me a really long time to come up with this and then when I did I had to wait a month to give it to you. Please can I give you your gift?" She pleaded.

"Oh all right, but only because you begged so prettily." I said trying to sound magnanimous. She snorted and swatted my arm then rolled over and pulled a wrapped box from under the bed. It was a huge box and I didn't know how she managed to pull it up onto the bed.

"It's patchwork wrapped." She shrugged. "I didn't have enough of any one kind of paper so I used a couple and patch worked it together."

I snorted, delighted that she would go to such trouble, "I love it. You sure you want me to open it?"

"Yes! Please, please, please open it! It's been driving me crazy!" I chuckled at her and started tearing off the paper. When I got to the very nondescript box I flashed her a curious look but opened the box.

There sitting amidst crumpled newspaper was an OEM Knucklehead Panhead WLA WLC Harley Solo Seat. It was in perfect condition and wrapped in plastic. It was beautiful and was embellished on the sides of the seat with medallions and it certainly looked comfortable, but I couldn't figure out why she would give it to me.

"This is beautiful Angel mama, thank you." I said honestly but maybe a bit confused.

"Don't worry, this is just part of it, the rest is at Alana's house because I couldn't hide it here." She laughed and it was the most beautiful sound I had ever heard.

"All right Angel mama, I suppose you'd like your gift now, too. You don't want to wait until midnight do you?"

"David, if you want to wait until midnight to give me my gift I am totally ok with that. It was just your gift that was driving me nuts. Of course now that you have that part waiting until you see the rest of it will also drive me nuts."

"Oh trust me baby, the wait for that will drive me nuts right along with you. How about I give you your gift and we can occupy ourselves somehow to keep our minds off of it."

"Oh, and how are we going to occupy ourselves?"

"I think we can come up with something." I said chuckling as I got off the bed and walked over to my closet. I reached into my duffle bag and pulled out the little black box I had hidden there. When I turned around so Brooke could see it she gasped and her eyes got wide. Yep, she's surprised.

Brooke

Oh my God! Is that a ring box? Please let that be a ring box!

"Brooke, Angel mama," David said, stepping back to the bed and kneeling in front of me. "I love you more than anything else in this world. You've blessed me with so much, will you marry me?" Before I could say anything I kissed him then stood up and pulled him to stand with me.

"David, I don't want you to ever feel like you have to beg me for anything. We are equals and I want you to feel confident that I will support you in every way and stand with you no matter what. I love you and you have blessed me with more than you could ever know. Yes, I will marry you." I said reaching up and kissing him again. He pulled back and opened the ring box, plucked out the most uniquely beautiful ring I had ever seen.

It was a round cut solitaire diamond with smaller diamonds placed on either side to look like angel wings all set in platinum. It was spectacular but even if it had been a plain gold band it would have been perfect. I stared at it for a long time and David must have gotten nervous when I didn't say anything.

"Do you like it? If you don't we can get another, I won't be hurt or upset. Is it too big or too small?"

I shook my head so hard I must have scattered my joyful tears across the room. "No David, I love it, it's perfect."

I threw myself at him, wrapping my arms around him and holding him tight. He laughed and held me though not too closely since my belly was in the way. I pulled back and kissed him, trying to pour into him all the love I felt for him with that kiss.

"Mmmmm," he hummed into my mouth then gasped when my hands slipped under his shirt and pushed it up and over his head. I kissed him hungrily again and attacked the snap on his jeans and pulled it apart and the zipper down, shoving them with his briefs down his hips and thighs. "Brooke..."

"Quiet David," I said, turning him and pushing him so he fell back on the bed. He chuckled as he bounced a little and I pulled off his boots and socks, yanking his pants right off his legs.

I loved his legs, they were thick with muscle and lightly dusted with crisp hair. My fiancé was a gorgeous specimen of manhood that was for sure. And speaking of his manhood, it stood at attention, waiting for me.

Once he was naked and I had whipped all of my clothes off I began to crawl up the bed towards his spectacular manhood and watched the desire flare in his eyes.

"Move up."

He did what I asked then let me position him the way I wanted him. I couldn't lay on my stomach as big as it was so I cocked his hip and bent his knee so I could rest against it and lie on my side and still reach his cock with my mouth.

I licked him from base to tip then sucked one of his balls into my mouth and squeezed his cock with my hand, stroking him as I kissed and licked him. He moaned and arched his hips a bit off the bed and panted.

I knew what he wanted but wouldn't ask me to do. I lifted up as high as I could and tilted the tip of his dick to my lips then slipped it past and into my wet mouth. I flattened my tongue on the underside of him and I took him deep and swallowed when I felt him bump the back of my throat.

"Angel baby stop . . . fuck that feels so good . . . baby please stop I don't want to cum in your mouth." I finally stopped, letting him fall out of my mouth with a pop. "Come up here baby, straddle me and ride me."

I sat astride him and took his cock in my hand and guided him into me, throwing my head back and whimpering at the complete feeling of fullness. It was so amazing this feeling.

David bracketed my hips with his big hands and helped lift me then pull me down on him with each of his upward thrusts. He was already primed to explode from me sucking him and once he started playing with my clit it didn't take me long to orgasm.

He thrust a few short quick pumps then pulled almost all the way out of me and slammed back in, sending me over the edge pulling him with me. When we had both come back to earth I collapsed beside him and he pulled me close to him.

"I love you." He whispered in my ear and rubbed my belly. I kissed him softly then fell asleep nestled in his protective warmth and strength.

CHAPTER 19
Axle

"David!" I could hear her voice but I just couldn't force myself to open my eyes. "David wake up! David, it's Christmas morning! You have to wake up, we have to go!"

"Isn't there a Christmas tradition of sleeping in?" I asked, my voice raspy from sleep.

"No David, it's almost eight and we have to be at the church by nine for mass. If we're lucky at this point we won't have to park four blocks away and stand at the back of the church." She was getting frantic so I took pity on her and got out of bed.

"I'll be ready in five minutes." I promised her with a kiss on the tip of her nose. I jumped in the shower and quickly washed up and brushed my teeth, calling over the noise of the water, "Are we meeting Lo and Alana and family at the church?"

"Yeah, they should be leaving any minute now. Alana promised to save us a spot but it's going to be hard." She griped. Just as she was about to tell me to hurry up I shut the water off and got out drying off. "That's not fair." She said pouting.

I laughed at her and pulled on the new dress pants and dress shirt she had bought me for today. She said my boots were nice enough if I polished them and the pants and shirt would look good under my leather jacket.

"Ready." I said standing in front of her.

"It took me an hour to get ready; you literally just got ready in less than ten minutes."

"Yeah, but you look a hell of a lot better than I do."

"Depends on who you ask," She said finger combing my hair back and straightening my collar.

"Let's go or we're going to be late." I teased her, swatting her butt. We rushed out to my truck and drove into town to the Cathedral and found a parking spot only a block from the church instead of four. We got lucky.

Alana and Lo were saving us a spot but it was tight. Drew ended up sitting on my lap and Alana's parents had to sit in the pew ahead of us. Not that they minded, they had been coming to this church for so many years they knew everyone here like family anyway.

The mass was beautiful and the choir was amazing. Afterwards we made our way back to Alana and Lo's much more sedately. Brooke said I had to park at the clubhouse so we could walk up to the house and was adamant about it. I gave her a strange look but acquiesced, if she wanted to walk home in the cold who was I to deny her that?

We walked up to the house hand in hand but when we got to the barn she stopped me smiling then tugged me into the barn.

"You know baby if you bought me a horse that seat won't fit on it right?" I asked, chuckling.

"I didn't buy you a horse, I bought you that." I looked to where she was pointing and was stunned speechless.

"Is that . . . ?"

"That is a 1945 Harley Davidson WLC. Obviously not in mint condition, but that was kind of the point. I thought maybe you would want to fix it up, the seat was just the first step." She shrugged.

"Baby, these go for $23,000, how did you afford this?"

"Oh, I know how much they are in much better shape than that. You know my parents and my grandparents left me some money. If the point of the gift had been a mint condition bike I could have paid for that but that wasn't the point. The point was a project and the shared history you have with this bike. No; you didn't fight in the war in 1945 and this bike has been long out of commission, but you both have a history of war. You both came home a little broken and in need of a little TLC."

"Angel mama, this is amazing. This is the best gift anyone has ever given me, thank you so much." I said pulling her into my arms and letting the tears slip down my cheeks unashamed that I was a grown man, battle hardened and crying like a baby. I pulled back from her and cupped her face in my palms, resting my forehead on hers. "Thank you."

"You're welcome." Brooke said smiling. "Now let's get inside, I'm freezing!"

I laughed at her and followed her the rest of the way to the house. As soon as we walked in the front door Alana and Kat attacked Brooke squealing and dancing around over her ring, then they did the same over Alana's new ring, copying the ritual they did when Hammer had asked Kat to marry him.

Lo walked over and shook my hand and we did that manly one armed bro hug that men do and wished each other a Merry Christmas. Alana, her mom Joann and Judy had laid out a huge buffet so the adults could eat and the kids could open their gifts and neither had to wait for the other.

I filled up a plate to share with Brooke then found her in the living room in a big arm chair and sat at her feet. I passed her the plate and she ate a few bits and gave it back to me, reaching every so often for a little more. She played with my hair as we watched Alana's kids have fun with their new toys.

My mom opened her gift from me that I had of course put Brooke's name on and gasped in delight. She thanked me profusely then showed off her tickets to everyone. Brooke had told everyone about my new to me bike and they had each gotten me new parts for it.

Brooke and Kat got a bunch of baby stuff and Alana got jewelry. Everyone was happy, even Seether who wasn't overly fond of Christmas but we had all pitched in to get him a new computer set up.

After we'd all eaten our fill and the kids had been sent to bed and Kat and Brooke were yawning every two minutes we decided to call it a night. I helped Brooke into her coat and we started walking back to the clubhouse.

Kat and Hammer followed close behind and Lo stayed behind for a few minutes to love on Alana a little bit before he too followed us once she promised to sneak out to his room later. Seether had gone ahead an hour or so ago to get a head start on setting up his new system.

Just as we got to the edge of the parking lot we were surprised by screeching tires and fired shots. Hammer and I pushed Kat and Brooke gently down to the ground and covered them with our bodies. We watched as a car slid to a stop in front of the gates of the compound, more shots were fired and something was shoved out the back door, then the door was slammed shut and the car sped off.

"Get the girls inside." Lo ordered as he rushed to see what was lying on the ground. Hammer and I lifted the girls off the ground and carried them inside, setting them just inside the door then running out with Seether fast on our heels. "What the fuck?"

"What is it Lo?" I demanded when we came to a stop beside him and the lump laying on the gathering snow.

"A body," he answered looking up at me. Just as we were all about to go into shock the body moaned and we all jumped in surprise.

"Shit, she's alive." Seether exclaimed crouching beside her. "We gotta get her inside." Carefully he lifted her off the ground and into his arms cradling her tight to his chest as she cried out in pain. "I'll put her in my room, Axle, get your mom."

"What? Why would I get my mom?"

"Because she's a nurse, nimrod," Seether said, hustling the girl inside. Shit I was dumb sometimes. Of course my mom was a nurse!

I rushed down the hall to the room she was using and knocked on her door. I was about to knock again harder when the door opened and my mom stood there in oversized men's flannel pajamas.

"What's wrong David?"

"Axle," I said automatically. "I mean, there was a body dumped out in front of the gate but the girl is alive, we need your help."

I didn't wait for an answer, just rushed away to get back to Seether's room. Brooke and Kat were there helping as much as they could but really as big as they were right now they were just in the way.

"Girls out, I need our help out in the hall more than in here where your bellies are in the way." My mom commanded, taking charge.

"Of course Edith," They both said with no hurt feelings.

"Boys, hot water, towels, bandages, antiseptic," mom just kept giving orders as she checked the girl over. "She needs to be in the hospital." At that the girl gripped mom's hand so tight I thought she was going to break her fingers. "Ok sweetie, no hospital, can you tell me if anything is broken?"

The girl shook her head again but slower as she dropped out of consciousness.

Brooke

I watched from the hall as Edith checked the girl over, looking for broken bones or cuts we couldn't see. At one point when Edith started to undress her, the girl started to completely lose it. We had all thought she was unconscious but she woke up pretty quick for that.

"Boys, get out," Edith commanded quietly then looked at Kat and I, "Lo call Alana. I'm sorry girls, I need some female help in here but you're both too big around the middle right now to be much help."

"It's okay Edith," Kat replied, shaking her head, tears slipping down her cheeks as Hammer hugged her to him. "We understand." Edith sighed heavily and stepped into the hall but left the door open.

"I suspect that given the way her clothes are disheveled, her pants are inside out and the snap undone, she's curled in the fetal position and clutching her stomach and with the way she reacted when I tried to undress her I'd say she's been raped, for sure beaten but rape wouldn't surprise me." Edith closed her eyes and let go of a shuddering breath then looked at Kat with such love in her eyes it was almost painful to see.

"I never told either of you this, and now is probably not the best time for it but I need you to understand why I let Matthew into our lives." Edith said wiping her own tears off her cheeks.

"Mom -," David started shaking his head.

"No David, you need to know. When you were fourteen I had found a gentleman friend and we went on a few dates. I thought he was a nice man but no one I was going to spend the rest of my life with. When I tried to break it off with him he raped me, he didn't beat me like someone did to that poor girl but rape is rape. As a result of that night I got pregnant and God gave me my beautiful Katherine."

"Mom -," Katherine whispered the despair in her voice hard to bear.

"You got me through those really tough nights Katherine, without you, knowing you were growing inside me gave me a reason to go on. And David you were so strong, so accomplished. I left you then, not physically but I left you and I am so sorry."

"Mom stop," David ordered, pulling his mother into his arms and holding her tightly against him. He heard Kat sob and he reached out and pulled her over as well. "This can wait, thank you for being so strong and brave to tell us this much mom. The rest we will do when we're sitting somewhere comfortable and there isn't a girl in that room barely alive."

"You're right David," Edith said, pulling away from her son again wiping the tears from her cheeks again, assuming that David was chastising her for her outbreak.

"Mom," he whispered, pulling her to him again. He cupped the back of her head with his hand and pushed his lips against her ear. I don't know what he said but it touched her deeply because she sobbed again and nodded then turned and went back to the girl in Seether's room.

Just then Alana burst into the hallway, "I'm here; what's the emergency?"

"Here baby," Lo said, guiding her into his arms and whispering in her ear what had happened since we left her house.

I couldn't watch any more as she broke down then composed herself, I fit myself against David's chest and buried my face against his throat and felt him swallow hard as though he were trying to control his emotions. He was braced with his hands against the wall and his head hanging but I didn't care, we needed to comfort each other.

I wrapped my arms around his waist and waited for him to do the same. After a few minutes he did and held me so tight I almost thought he was going to cut off my oxygen.

"Let's go to bed, your mom will take care of her with Alana and Lo. Let's see if we can get some sleep." I murmured to him, feeling him nod and allowed me to lead him to our room.

He sat on our bed for a minute with his elbows on his knees and his head in his hands. For once my cat was in the room and lying on his pillow like the king he believed he was. I tried to shoo him away as I got undressed and ready for bed but he ignored me.

"It's all right Angel the cat can stay for now." David said rubbing his hands over his face. "I'm sorry about that."

"Why, because you have emotions and feelings and you're not made of stone?" I asked almost scathingly. "Don't be sorry for that David, I love that about you. You aren't afraid to feel."

He smiled slightly and sighed then pulled his shirt over his head and tossed it towards the laundry hamper in the bathroom. I scowled at it and he chuckled lightly then got up and put the shirt in the hamper.

"Thank you." I said, gifting him with a smile.

"Anything for you Angel mama." He replied, wrapping his arms around my waist and kissing me sweetly.

"Tell me about your dad?" I asked, smoothing my fingers over his slightly scruffy cheeks.

"Hmmm, let's get into bed." He said, pulling away from me to take his pants off.

I thought that meant he wouldn't tell me anything, since he had never brought his dad up before I didn't think they had a very good relationship and I knew nothing about the man. I was wrong though; as soon as we were comfortable David started to talk.

"My dad was amazing," He said quietly then chuckled. "He was the best dad a boy could ever ask for. We played baseball and hockey and football, he was at every game and picked me up from every practice. He was stern but gentle and caring and loving and compassionate. Everything a little boy could ever want or need. And he was often indulgent which drove my mom nuts. He was a cop and he was on duty a lot so often he showed up to those practices and games in his uniform with his patrol car. He didn't or couldn't always stay for the whole game but he tried.

"Then one day he was gone. I was ten and his partner showed up at our door and I didn't hear what he said but I watched my mom crumple to the floor screaming that Grant was wrong and my dad was coming home like always as soon as his shift ended. Grant just shook his head and stepped back letting our pastor take over with her. She was a zombie for years. That time she was talking about when I was fourteen was the happiest I had seen her since before my dad died. That it ended the way it did kills me, and I didn't even know about it."

"David, you're not to blame and you're not responsible for what that man did to your mom. Because you didn't now doesn't make it your fault. You were just a little boy, even at fourteen"

"I know, I do and I'm ok, we got Kat out of the whole ordeal but it still hurts."

"I know baby," I kissed him softly on his lips trying only to console him and before I knew it I was on my back and he was making love to me so sweetly I almost cried it was so perfect. We orgasmed together almost gently and then fell asleep wrapped up in each other.

CHAPTER 20

Axle

When I woke up the next morning Brooke was still sleeping soundly so I snuck quietly out of bed and left her to sleep. When I got to the kitchen Lo and Alana were there looking exhausted and shell shocked. Kat and Hammer were also in the kitchen but looked much more rested.

"Did you guys get any sleep at all?" I asked, pouring myself a cup of coffee. Alana shook her head no and Lo answered, "Not much."

"Is the girl ok?" Hammer asked wrapping one of his massive mitts around his coffee cup.

"Nothing's broken," Alana sighed "But Edith was right, she was raped and kicked so hard in the stomach that the bruises are boot prints on her skin. She probably has a concussion and the bruises aren't just on her stomach, they're all over her body and it looks like she was likely beaten by more than one person."

We all sat quietly for a moment before Lo stood up and punched a huge dent in the fridge before he stormed out of the room. Alana looked at us sheepishly but we just shook our heads at her.

"Why don't you go get some sleep," Kat said to her kindly. "Mom's gone to bed, Seether's sitting with the girl, we'll let you all know if she wakes up or says anything." Alana nodded and sniffed then got up and followed Lo out of the room. "Who could have done this to her?"

"Little D." Both Hammer and I said at the same time.

"That was his vanity plate, L'il D." Hammer added, rubbing his hand up and down Kat's back. "We gotta put an end to this soon. He's already threatened our women and our children and if that's what he does to women then none of them are safe."

"You're right, we gotta get Seether on this right away." I said standing and leaving the room. I found Seether sitting in the computer chair in his room staring at the girl in his room. "We need you to work your magic man."

"No," he replied, not lifting his eyes from his bed.

"Seether man, you gotta find this douche. We have a make and model now of his vehicle. He did this to her, find him for her so we can put him down." I ground out between my teeth.

I was being purposely harsh because I knew that would get Seether's blood pumping and he wouldn't rest until he found Little D and possibly killed the little fucker himself.

Printed in Great Britain
by Amazon